Life
Sciences

JOY SORMAN

Translated from the French by Lara Vergnaud
Introduction by Catherine Lacey

RESTLESS BOOKS
Brooklyn, New York

This is a work of fiction. Names, characters, places, and incidents herein are either the products of the author's imagination or are used fictitiously. Any resemblance to actual events or persons, living or dead, is entirely coincidental.

Copyright © 2017 Editions du Seuil
Translation copyright © 2021 Lara Vergnaud
Introduction copyright © 2021 Catherine Lacey

First published as *Sciences de la vie* by Editions du Seuil, Paris, 2017

First Restless Books paperback edition October 2021

Paperback ISBN: 9781632062956
Library of Congress Control Number: 2021937473

This work received the French Voices Award for excellence in publication and translation. French Voices is a program created and funded by the French Embassy in the United States and FACE (French American Cultural Exchange).

This book is supported in part by an award from the National Endowment for the Arts.

NATIONAL
ENDOWMENT for the ARTS
========================= arts.gov

Cover design by Keenan
Text design by Sarah Schneider
French Voices Logo designed by Serge Bloch

Printed in the United States of America

1 3 5 7 9 10 8 6 4 2

Restless Books, Inc.
232 3rd Street, Suite A101
Brooklyn, NY 11215

www.restlessbooks.org
publisher@restlessbooks.org

"A story of self-empowerment, this 'medical carousel' is neither dramatic nor maudlin. It is rather a Kafkaesque struggle against determinism, atavism, and unwanted family legacies."

—Laila Maalouf, *La Presse*

"*Life Sciences* can also be read as a coming-of-age tale about the possibility of freeing oneself from hereditary afflictions, even from the constraints of womanhood. It is an allegory, but of what? We can't be sure. All the better; it is up to the reader to choose the prognosis."

—Grégoire Leménager, *L'Obs*

"As Joy Sorman brings to life a young heroine struck by a hereditary curse, she creates a jubilant bildungsroman, an ode to life itself. . . . It is her best novel to date."

—Sean James Rose, *Livres Hebdo*

"There is something visceral in Joy Sorman's writing. It reeks of sweat, effort, physical suffering, and bestiality."

—Flavie Gauthier, *Le Soir*

"Sorman's subtle writing is in itself a paradox: it is both extremely precise, particularly in scientific contexts, and extremely sensual."   **—Hubert Prolongeau, *Marianne***

INTRODUCTION

Women are heiresses, inheritors of a thousand demented and limiting ideas of what a woman can or should be. Most women know this; many resist. And while some will say this is a battle waged between the sexes, the keen will know that feminism is an act against history itself. And yet, at times a feminist might wonder—where and when in history did this hostile subjugation begin? And why?

It is possible this oppression did not begin as an abstract hatred for the female sex, but in a sheer terror of bodily decay. Centuries of men have been trying to avoid the unfathomable fact of death by exaggerating every unfathomable aspect of the feminine form. *Never trust anyone who bleeds for a week without dying*, the old joke goes, a desperate stab to belittle the fleshy origin of all men.

Though Ninon Moise, heroine of this wonderfully modern and timeless fable, *Life Sciences*, is able to trace her particular doom through the genes in her maternal lineage, knowing where her suffering comes from does not offer relief. Torturous pains and unexplainable maladies flow from generation to generation in her family—"a string of genetic catastrophes." Like all the women who've come before them, Ninon and her mother (who was lucky enough *only* to be struck by a form of blindness) are so wedded to the inevitability of their suffering that its anticipation ultimately guarantees its arrival. This stance—this bracing for an unreasonable inevitability—will be familiar to anyone who has lived through girlhood.

Every girl reaches a point in her childhood (perhaps the end of her childhood) when she perceives the approaching tsunami. What's more, we gladly prepare these girls to live within the historic limits of the feminine: how to be pretty, to be nice, to be small, and most importantly—how to anticipate the violence looming over all that pretty, nice smallness. Fairy tales tell this again and again—there is a place for you in this world, a beautiful and dangerous place, and it's better that you accept it now as you really have no choice. Better to prepare girls for what's coming, no? Better to tell them the bad news first, and let them invent their own good news later.

From a young age, the stories of Ninon's doomed female lineage serve as her bedtime stories—from Marie Lacaze's dancing fits in 1518 to Catherine Tendron's witchy seizures, to Ninon's own grandmother, Louise, who abruptly went deaf and blind at fifteen for no known reason. Soon, none of her children's books will appease the serious Ninon. She only wants stories of the curse, and she studies her body in wait of what will soon consume it.

Children who immediately prefer the true, bad news over the soothing fantasy are often disturbing to adults. They seem to know too much, too quickly, as they readily discard the soft blinders of childhood. Our heroine is just such a child, and perhaps because she is so enamored with the dark fairy tale she's been told will define her life, her version of the curse is a particularly painful, unlivable one. In this way, perhaps *Life Sciences* is a cautionary tale— fall in love with the stories you're told, and they will be that much harder to change.

A series of doctors—most of them nonplussed and male—shrug at Ninon. They live in the limits of their own stories, in particular the belief that their knowledge of the human body is complete, and that female pain is trivial. Her troubles are "nothing life-threatening," one of them tells Ninon, all while her excruciating pain encases her life in threat. Even when a diagnosis arrives, these ambivalent professionals still insist: "It's not serious, it's mysterious, it's trying, it's rare, but you don't die from it, it's being researched, a little, it's not very profitable yet, but still, people are interested in it, kind of."

The word *unfathomable* appears only once in this feminist *Metamorphosis*, but it feels especially pertinent to its concerns. Truly, the condition of being mortal, regardless of gender, is at least in some respects an unfathomable experience, and it is through story that we try to fathom our way through it. For centuries, men have written an ever-limiting set of stories about women, and the project of un-telling those old stories is a relatively recent development. Women so often carry this delusion of being innately *wrong*, of needing to be numbed, controlled, caged or hidden—a delusion smuggled into us in the Trojan horse of a thousand old stories.

The way out of this cycle, Joy Sorman suggests, is the same way we got into it: "No experience is pure, no experience exists without a story," she writes. We must tell stories like this one. We must read stories like this one, an honest cure.

CATHERINE LACEY
Chicago, April 2021

Life Sciences

"All that lives in me is my life."

Werner Herzog
The Enigma of Kaspar Hauser

Ninon Moise's family is cursed, forever branded by infamy and infection, a fate as ludicrous as it is tragic, the notion of transmission and of contamination alike, a string of genetic catastrophes, generation after generation: accounts of disease, evil spells, madness and bewitchings, a multitude of ills that have systematically struck the eldest daughters since the sixteenth century.

Ninon Moise's family tree is a history of France and pathology as shown by a myriad of extraordinary medical cases—a proliferating misfortune that, from 1518 to the 2010s, mutated with every birth, like a virus always faster than the humans it poisons, faster than progress or science. You can search all you want for good health or reason in the cracks of this family saga, there's no point, all the female ancestors are mad or sick, affected in one way or another. This calamity never stopped or even slowed the bloodline, or discouraged anyone from having children, thereby perpetuating a centuries-old joke. Was this stupid and selfish blindness or, on the contrary, blissful indifference, confidence in the future and in life, in the very principle of life, meaning movement, regeneration, and opposing forces?

Young Ninon Moise is the heroine and last-born of this family that has methodically deteriorated through the centuries, heir to an imposing genetic legacy, and perhaps, who knows, the final link in the chain, the end of an ill-fated lineage.

The first mention of this family malediction, the starting point for a series of clinical metamorphoses—the meticulous recording of which has never been interrupted—and undoubtedly also wild modifications to DNA sequences, can be found in the archives of the city of Strasbourg: a case of dancing plague that struck in the summer of 1518 and whose patient zero is named Marie Lacaze, a thirty-one-year-old embroiderer married to a blacksmith-farrier, mother of three, no known medical history.

On the morning of July 14, Marie awakens in an odd state, like she's charged with electricity—pins and needles in her hands and feet, shooting pain in her lower abdomen, a warm sensation on the nape of her neck, buzzing in her ears, the hairs on the back of her head standing on end.

A kink in the body that over the course of several minutes takes complete control of Marie, visibly worsens and degenerates: she begins to wriggle for no reason in front of her incredulous husband and children, jumping and letting out high-pitched cries as though the ground was covered with embers.

Then Marie Lacaze streaks out of her house in her nightgown and begins furiously striding up and down the town streets, followed by her powerless husband who doesn't dare touch her for fear that she's possessed.

Marie dances, frenzied, without pause, nothing can stop her it seems, she circles the village like this several times, feet bloody and raw, she's pale, dripping sweat, her face worn by fatigue, dark rings under her eyes, her body no longer belongs to her, she keeps dancing, flailing her arms, lifting her knees, spinning around, she falls but gets right back up to resume her dance, and so on for five days and five nights, desperately mute.

But before long Marie is no longer alone, joined at sunrise by other dancers taken by the same fever, and soon they are fifty in the streets of Strasbourg, then two hundred, and by the fifth day, four hundred and fifty women, men, and even children, more and more curious onlookers as well, who come to watch the spectacle of madmen with beseeching, bloodshot gazes: faces deformed by pain, fingers stiffened by god knows what poison, they moan in anguish, pleading for help with eyes rolling back into their heads, there's nothing joyful about their frenetic and jerky dance, terror has taken over the town, its residents stay inside for fear of being contaminated in turn. The trance spreads like a plague, many end up collapsing, out of breath, from mental and physical exhaustion, their bodies on the ground still shaken by spasms, some die: heart attack, broken neck, dehydration, and the unafflicted hasten to burn the contagious, or at the least sullied, remains of these creatures of the devil.

On the fifth day, the Strasbourg town council finally decides to take action and has the brilliant and absurd idea of hiring professional musicians to accompany the dance, hoping to transform madness into celebration—because what could be more normal than dancing to the sound of tambourins, bells, and viols? Platforms are erected throughout the town, different orchestras alternate, and in three days the sickness is eradicated, the abnormal movements stop, the anarchical and violent gesticulations become harmonious and fluid, melody runs through the villagers' veins like an antidote, bodies slow and then stand still; Marie Lacaze is one of the first to get better, her pulse returns to normal, her arms go limp, then her legs relax, a few final pas de bourrées, and her entire body finds itself at rest, delivered.

Marie will never fully recover, suffering from cramps, asthma, tingling in her limbs, and anxiety attacks; unable to tolerate the slightest musical note—even her children's melodious babbling will trigger unbearable pain.

The origins of this episode of dancing mania have never been explained, though several hypotheses circulated, none of which really stuck: poisoning by mycotoxin-contaminated rye, a heretical ceremony, unfavorable alignment of the stars, collective hysteria among weak individuals prone to superstition and, by extension, madness. Because most of the victims came from modest backgrounds, certain doctors took that as proof that the poor are more sheeplike than others, thus more susceptible to waves of panic. It was also noted that, in previous years, a series of epidemics and famines had struck Strasbourg and left its inhabitants vulnerable and anxious—conditions were therefore ripe.

Long afterward, some suggested the possibility of Sydenham chorea or Huntington's disease, also called Saint Vitus's dance, a nervous disorder that causes meningeal congestion and is characterized by awkward and involuntary limb movements, generalized agitation, muscular contractions, and digestive problems; but how could this type of streptococcal inflammation have affected Marie Lacaze and then spread?

*

From a very young age, Ninon Moise is told this story, family legend and foundational myth, by her mother, Esther Moise, Marie's distant descendant, with a mix of sincere pride and feigned distress.

It's the '90s, Ninon doesn't care about the adventures of Little Brown Bear or the Papa Beaver series, only this breed of incredible account can calm her childish excitement, keep her attention at bedtime, and soon she begins to demand, every night, the tale of Marie Lacaze, that primogenitor lost to the ages, reduced to parchment paper in the Strasbourg archives, the crown of the family tree, patient zero and ancestress zero. Marie Lacaze is hero and monster, the gene that mutated, and five centuries later, the family's pride and despair still reside in her.

After Marie Lacaze, first of the lineage, there are plenty more never-before-heard stories to tell the impatient but attentive child, eyes wide, tucked in bed, all her picture books permanently relegated to the storage unit—a nocturnal ritual that sets the rhythm to Ninon's childhood, a paradise populated with magical tales, fervently animated by Esther, who likes nothing better than to unroll the endless ribbon of the genealogical fable: and so through the centuries, there are cases of trance and insanity, visual and auditory hallucinations, mental disorders and uterine aggressions treated with trepanning and bleedings, bodies that escape, overflow, rave, noted in the family records as the epiphenomena or aftershocks of Marie's initial madness, but also stories of hunchbacks, epilepsy, aphasia, somnambulism, scabies, sudden limb deformations, a girl born with one ear, or the peasant woman with a particularly developed sense of smell who thinks she's a dog, yet another one born with an exaggerated cleft palate that leaves her with a rasping voice, countless injurious genes, hair that falls out completely in the span of one night or goes gray in one hour, a third breast sprouting from the abdomen, nails and teeth that crumble like sand and never grow back, eyes that change color, a bearded woman, unexpected muscle weakness, abnormal digestive issues, unexplained bradycardia, varied protuberances, and even small horns growing out of the skull, piercing the scalp, that need to be filed regularly.

Esther recounts these episodes with such dramatic glee and theatricality that little Ninon, awestruck, very rapidly becomes aware that she carries sickness inside her like a ticking time bomb. From the first stories her mother tells in the soothing light of the bedside lamp, the child is on the lookout for signs of the hereditary curse, in her stomach mostly, attentive to any rumblings, but also scrutinizing her head, hands, feet, then, later, worrying about urine that is too pale, a dry and saburral tongue, a pallid complexion— and could this slight dizziness, this eczema, this fever, this tingling augur a more serious malady? Her mother doesn't appear overly concerned about the negative effects these accounts might have on such a friable young individual, and seems to take it for granted that no descendant of Marie

Lacaze of Strasbourg can escape the sickness, the only questions being its nature and form, and at what moment it will manifest.

This sickness, transmitted by the mother, by her mother, who's raising her alone—Ninon was conceived one New Year's Eve with the cooperation of a drunk stranger who took off shortly after the clock struck twelve—is perceived by the child as an object of both worry and desire, all the while being completely incorporated into her daily existence, seeing as it is a family tradition, and she is the only daughter, meaning the eldest daughter, the favored target. They're waiting for it to reveal itself like a divine gift and, in the meantime, the child can't help but devise hypotheses, observing that, for now, the integrity of both her mind and body appear indisputable.

Of course some hereditary anomalies remain latent, forever unbeknownst to their hosts, like inactive physical predispositions, but that was never the case in this family, their predispositions always made an appearance, due perhaps, on each occasion, to a random event, encounter, confrontation with the difficulties of life, but who can say for sure?

At the end of this hereditary chain begun in 1518, just before the last known link—Ninon—stands Esther Moise, who incarnates in her turn the extraordinary affliction linking all the family's eldest daughters across time. Esther inherits a form of ocular degeneration, achromatopsia: color blindness caused by the disappearance of the retina's visual pigments. Over the years, her vision, partial and obstructed, has been reduced to shades of gray, and her eyes have grown increasingly sensitive to light—at sixteen, she lost all color for good. Doctors diagnosed her early on, with the vague satisfaction felt upon coming across an unusual but nonetheless irrefutable case, a case that is observed but not explained.

Esther is therefore an anomaly, as were most of her ancestresses, samples to observe on a glass slide and place beneath a microscope, to grind into powder at the bottom of a test tube, to isolate in a sterile environment, to be framed by an entomologist, to dissect on a laboratory work bench, to conserve in a jar of formaldehyde, and to display in a window in the Museum of Medicine. In the great hereditary lottery, Ester Moise won the disease of reduced sight and immediately had the thought that fate could have been much crueler. She adapted to her disability, grew up with it, not particularly upset, was exempted from certain requirements at school, which made her special in her classmates' eyes, and then developed her professional life accordingly, becoming a projectionist in an art house cinema on the Rue des Écoles, working exclusively with old black-and-white movies, after getting a degree in cinema studies and certification as a film projectionist.

Esther is indifferent to Pixar animated films and superhero blockbusters and, apart from those two exceptions, considers black and white appropriate for all movies, and for that matter life, which doesn't really require color and light but rather movement and feeling. This night work is a good fit for her photophobia in the same way that cinema is a good fit for her unrelenting thirst for stories, and her tinted glasses, which she only takes off once evening falls, give her a movie-star allure that still never fails. It's in dimness that she truly becomes alive, a nocturnal animal fleeing the sun's rays, squinting her eyes behind her dark lenses to get them accustomed to the light, moving with increased ease and fluidity as the darkness swells, reborn at dusk, guided by her scotopic vision when the average person would fumble along, carrying a flashlight.

During the day, when her daughter is at school, Esther stays inside for hours on end, the shades drawn, sleeping, or listening to the radio and smoking cigarettes. At night, after her last showing, she doesn't come directly home, sometimes she gets a babysitter to stay with her child until early morning, walks around Paris, has random encounters in bars that cater to insomniacs, buys warm croissants when the bakery opens, and returns to wake up Ninon. The men who wander into her nights fall in love the instant she takes off her glasses, or puts them back on—the way she crinkles her eyes, lowering her lids over dark blue pupils, is irresistible.

Now, though Ninon's grown, and despite getting older herself, Esther's habits have barely changed, just slowed down a little—films, night, joyful roaming.

Besides the warm croissants, having an achromatic mother offers at least two advantages: the freedom to choose clothing in garish colors, mauve or turquoise for example, with complete impunity, and to match them any which way, and the daily treat of one or even several stories at bedtime, when other parents blame fatigue and seek a bit of rest and silence. And so Ninon finds herself entitled to different and more or less far-fetched versions of her mother's achromatopsia, one of which piques her interest in particular: the legend of the atoll of Pingelap, presented as one possible origin of Esther's pathology. The story goes that a great many of the two hundred and fifty inhabitants of this small piece of the Caroline Islands archipelago suffer from achromatopsia. This affliction, called *maskun* in the local language, has menaced all the island's families since the 1820s. According to legend, a pregnant woman was the source of the epidemic: she had gotten into the habit of walking along the beach each day under a blinding sun without taking any precautions, and the eyes of the child she was carrying were supposedly burnt by the light. That original injury, coupled with extensive consanguinity, went on to wreak havoc.

This careless mother who exposed her belly to the sun's deadly rays quickly joins the sorceresses and possessed women who populate Ninon's childhood imagination.

Ninon Moise turns three, seven, eleven, doesn't suffer from any ailments, no disease has manifested, nothing suspicious, a rather cheerful child, lulled by baleful and comical accounts, though she's somewhat solitary, like her mother, the solitude of a little girl whose head is full of tales as captivating as they are burdensome, whose heart sometimes tightens in worry—when will misfortune strike? what will its name be?—though she's also awaiting it with some excitement.

Ninon isn't traumatized by these cruel stories, didn't grow up any faster from hearing them, or any slower, just a little more alert than other children her age, forever waiting for a sign, monitoring her own body, an interior sentinel. Of course this attentiveness sometimes prompts bouts of hypochondria, but most often she floats carefree in a cloudy zone where the fictions told by her mother blend with real life, with life waiting to be lived.

Ninon is seventeen, in her final year at Lycée Jules-Ferry, in Paris's Place de Clichy, on the literature track, she'll take her final exams soon, lives with her mother in a three-room Hausmannian building on the Rue des Dames; she's gone through puberty, is fairly average, five feet four, 120 pounds, 34A, some acne, unwanted hair tamed, a brunette, girlfriends, acceptable grades, the occasional swim, movie theater, mall, cigarette, vodka-OJ, parties and stolen kisses, nothing more. Average, reserved, ordinary looking, sometimes to the despair of a mother who's secretly waiting for Ninon to be chosen, a mother who could be judged as misguided, reckless even, torn between the relief of knowing her daughter to be in good health and the impatience of seeing her struck in her turn, curious to learn what fate and the inexhaustible resources of the genome have in store for her. Esther Moise always told Ninon her genealogical sagas with such enthusiasm, irrigating her daughter's young malleable and porous brain with legends, because she herself had never been unhappy or overburdened by the disease that struck her, awareness of her uniqueness largely making up for the diminishment of her faculties—to the point that one could suspect her of having wanted to get sick, to be anointed by sickness, join an extraordinary lineage, remove herself from the anonymous masses, and have a destiny, consolations in which Ester Moise had always taken pride.

It's therefore time for her daughter to stand out, and it's as though that distinctiveness can only be revealed through her genes, as though uniqueness can only be expressed by a cell line, as though the force of a person's existence is resorbed whole by the transmission of genetic characteristics hoped to be rare and mysterious, as though that force can't be incarnated, for example, by an act—if her daughter were to contemplate climbing Everest without oxygen, Esther Moise would undoubtedly feel no surprise, no joy, not even worry.

No warning sign will be detected, no alert, no malfunction or change in Ninon's general state able to signal the affliction that finally strikes. If this affliction had been discreetly advancing through the silence and obscurity of her organs, she hadn't heard it. No notable event either, no trauma or accident liable to have triggered the disease. That's how it is, today's the day, you need a beginning, a date, an age, it's a January nineteenth, in the morning when she wakes up. It won't be gradual, it won't be underlying then exponential until it fully manifests; the anomaly and the pain are absent from her body on January eighteenth, and present the nineteenth, revealed, and when her troubling and unusual symptoms appear, Ninon quickly understands that this is it, the thing she can no longer name now that she's the host, the object, she knows perfectly well that this malady didn't land on her randomly, that it didn't come out of nowhere, but from a slowly formed bed of history and time, from layers of pathological strata—so, on this nineteenth of January, in the morning, existence as she knows it suddenly vanishes, an underground life takes power, the hereditary poison spreads through her body.

Normally it's the Rihanna ringtone on her cellphone—*Bitch better have my money*—that wakes her at 7:00 a.m., but this morning she opened her eyes a little earlier, the bluish screen indicates 6:39 and it's a feeling of uncustomary discomfort, of irritation and soon pain that pulls her from her sleep, like a bad dream that leaves a bitter aftertaste and crust in the eyes, a disagreeable posture that stiffens the body during the night, an inflammation of the nerves of the kind brought on by stormy weather. It takes Ninon a few seconds to emerge from this disagreeable torpor, a few seconds for body and mind to reconnect, crackling, for her bedroom to take form again—south-facing window, gray carpet, an Ikea desk in light pine—and then comes the urgent, imposing sensation of the sheet on her skin.

Lying in the fetal position, body huddled up beneath the comforter, Ninon is wearing pajama pants and a tank top, and the contact of the sheet on her naked, exposed arms is extraordinary, she can't feel anything else, it weighs heavy (lead), it burns (acid), it chafes (sandpaper), her two pained arms seem enormous to her, a brutal, crazy, impossible sensation that matches nothing she's ever known.

In a burst of panic, Ninon jumps out of her bed like it's on fire, rolls onto the carpet, which likewise burns her skin, lays still on her back, holds her arms above her, prepared to find them red, scratched, bleeding maybe, her skin raw, flayed, but nothing, the epidermis is smooth and white and the pain recedes as quickly as it appeared, like a hallucination gone without a trace.

Ninon brushes her fingers along the inside of her left arm, then the outside, slowly sweeps down from shoulder to hand then back up again, does the same on the right arm with extreme caution, hyper alert, but only feels slight pressure, a light stroke, really nothing abnormal, nothing violent. And yet she has no doubts about what just happened, about what her body just experienced. Ninon knows she wasn't dreaming; still lying on her back, she bravely grabs a T-shirt rolled into a ball from the foot of her bed, brings it closer with some apprehension and rubs it delicately against her forearm: at the first contact of cotton with her body she lets out a cry of surprise and pain, the fire is back, biting, she drops the shirt, then, still on the ground, picks up everything within reach, wool sock, canvas knapsack, stuffed unicorn, crumpled piece of paper, leather pencil case, each time brings the object to her skin, places it gently against one arm or the other, and it's always the same electric shock, the same venom, which evaporates as soon as the contact ends. Her arms remain intact to the naked eye, her skin barely reddens, the pain fades away, leaving no aura.

Before the strangeness and scale of what's happening, Ninon doesn't hesitate, it's irrefutable: the inescapable family affliction has just struck like lightning.

Ninon sits up, now cross-legged in the dark, her alarm will go off soon, there's a taste of earth and dread in her mouth.

She stands up, goes to awaken her mother who, seeing her in black and white and in tears, face ravaged by worry, shaken by spasms, eyes huge, immediately understands, filled with the same certainty as her daughter, the irreversible violence of the moment, the curse has begun, and knows herself incapable of reassuring or consoling Ninon.

What is this miserable conviction that keeps Esther and her daughter from considering, for even a second, that they are dealing with a temporary ailment, a momentary affliction, or even a fate dealt at random, from considering it as anything but a sign of the devil's work? In truth, they are so prepped, so conditioned, so possessed, that no doubt is allowed.

Mom, touch my arm, put your hand there, on my skin, please be gentle, just one finger, here, don't be scared, go ahead, and Esther, sitting up in her bed as her daughter stands in front of her speaking in a hollow, rushed voice, which has fallen an octave, fallen into a chasm, slowly extends her hand, touches the flesh in the crook of Ninon's elbow, applying pressure with one index finger. Ninon grimaces from the pain, stifles a little scream, a bird being strangled. Ninon is beside herself, a surge of hatred, a volley of lead shots to the heart, anger against Esther who is instantly judged guilty, an anger that swells, fills the space in the room and in her belly, a cooling liquid that freezes her arteries, and the child who so loved hearing stories of her ancestors disintegrates all at once—a small pile of sand at her mother's feet. Ninon storms out of Esther's bedroom, locks herself in the bathroom, rapidly undresses in front of the full-length mirror, begins to evaluate every inch of her body, to evaluate the extent of the damage, expects her skin to fall off, to crumble like dried earth; she grabs a towel, grazes, dabs, then rubs her feet, calves, thighs, stomach, back, neck, chest, butt, she feels nothing, not the slightest spark, her hands are unscathed too. This brings a fleeting sense of relief—so it only affects her arms, more precisely the area between her shoulders and wrists, inner and outer sides, right and left with equal intensity, the nightmare is confined, at least that's something.

But panic is quick to grab hold of her again, her thoughts racing at full speed, chaotic, Ninon is overwhelmed, incapable of reasoning against her fear, of slowing her heart, everything is blurring and spinning, she thinks of the wind and sun—will I still feel the softness of the wind and sun on my arms?—then she thinks about boys, that she's never had sex, about Tom whom she likes, with whom she imagined it could happen, she thinks that an operation might be conceivable, they'll remove patches of skin from her stomach or her back for example, to graft onto her two arms, to fix her, like how they graft burn victims, they'll grow stem cells from her epidermis to create thin, narrow skin sleeves that will cover her other skin, her sick, degenerating skin, and everything will go back to normal.

Ninon tries to calm her heart palpitations, runs water from the sink over her arms, hoping the liquid will be soothing, but it's the same sting, fear returns with a vengeance, she watches the trickle of water drip down her arm like a furrow of molten metal.

Then her skin dries, the pain quiets, she sniffs her arms like a worried animal looking for, expecting, an odor of rot, an odor of death, but her skin remains distressingly neutral, a homogenous, indifferent surface, until Ninon places a corner of the towel on it, presses gently, and then the pain gushes out from some unimaginable depth, as though the flesh of her arms wanted to pierce the thin outer membrane of her body, as though she was being hollowed down to the bone, a salvo of fire, the nerves on the inside like stripped electrical wires, a short circuit, the mind blinking off and on.

Esther is waiting at the kitchen table, breakfast is ready, Ninon joins her, they're sitting in silence, in a daze; they avoid eye contact, exaggeratedly stir their café au lait, contemplate the madeleine crumbs floating on the surface of the thick liquid; Ninon, whose hate has receded, finally says, in a barely audible voice, that maybe it's not so bad after all, that it must be treatable, her mother lifts her head, doesn't look so proud of her monstrous family now, I'm sorry, it's not what I imagined.

The daughter thinks the mother's crazy, a little off, maybe even dangerous.

At this point Ninon's wondering, nose in her mug, if the hypersensitivity of her skin—it seems like you could describe her symptom that way—which in this instant she names the "thing," the "thing" I have on my arms, has a medical definition; and in wondering this she regains a little courage, wants to see a doctor as soon as possible, is already hoping to recover before she's been officially declared sick. Ninon knows that the medical world has often revealed its impotence when faced with her family's dubious pathologies, practicing an "expectant medicine" that essentially lets nature take its course, but soon, once the shock has worn off, she will be determined to change the order of things.

It's nine a.m., Esther requests an urgent appointment with the neighborhood doctor, Dr. Fillet, a man in his fifties with a waxy complexion and impeccable nails; Ninon insists on going alone, slips a long jacket that burns her skin over her pajama bottoms and her tank top.

She spends twenty minutes in the waiting room—lifeless walls, posters of landscapes, frayed sofas—before being seen by the jaded but affable doctor in a checkered shirt who doesn't have time to ask her what's wrong, what brings her in, because Ninon bursts into tears before she can say a word, the disconcerted doctor hands her a box of tissues, waits until it's over, looking away, visually tracing a crack in one wall, while Ninon tries to calm down, apologizes, sniffs, make partial sentences, I'm here because there's something wrong with my skin, I can't bear physical contact, any contact at all with my arms, it feels like burning, even water burns, I can't be touched anymore, I can't wear clothes anymore, it's excruciatingly painful, what is it?

The doctor hesitates for a moment, furrows his brows, summoning a lion's wrinkle between his eyes, asks in an artificially detached tone what happened, if other symptoms appeared, if an unusual event recently occurred, if Ninon experienced some kind of shock, if she has a fever, a migraine, vomiting, if there are family antecedents, allergies, cancers, if she's depressed, what she ate yesterday, if she drank alcohol, took drugs, if she fell, if she had a prolonged tanning session, put any cream whatsoever on her arms, takes birth control or other medication: the answer to all these questions is negative and Ninon shakes her head sadly.

But the most surprising part is that she doesn't mention her family's pathological history, of which she is the newest chapter, says nothing about this element that seems insignificant at this point—does she sense that to break the cursed chain she must remain silent, isolate her case and entrust it to medicine, to not interpret the pain but settle for treating it?

The doctor doesn't need to know, the information would be of no use to him, it could even prove to be deleterious, lead him down the wrong path, cloud his judgment. And while Ninon's family is somewhat more so than others, it's understood that every family is pathogenic so what's the point in stating it.

Dr. Fillet asks Ninon to lie down on the examining table, rubs in some hand sanitizer, pushes up his shirtsleeves, applies light pressure to various spots on her arms, each time provoking a grimace of pain, yes that hurts, there, and there too, everywhere, he stops and the pain disappears instantly; he doesn't insist, instead palpates her stomach, checks her ears, tongue, the back of her throat, her reflexes, blood pressure, a little low, and ends the exam by listening to her heart—he likes this particular moment of the auscultation, capturing the delicate noises of the heart muscle and the deployment of the alveoli, the internal whispers and murmurs, miniscule movements, bodily acoustics that he receives in tense concentration. But this attentive listening to Ninon's heart doesn't tell him anything more about this odd case that leaves him powerless, with no clinical hypothesis, with no remedies to suggest.

Dr. Fillet doesn't doubt Ninon Moise, doesn't think her pain is imaginary, but it's not within his capabilities, he tells her, adds that this falls under a specialist's competencies, that it requires testing, searching, going deeper, for an opinion to be reached; Ninon, who has been an emotional mess for two hours, feels desperate, you can't leave me in this state, tears are welling beneath her eyelids, the doctor suggests an anxiolytic injection, that's all I have in my power for the moment, it will make you less anxious and no doubt calm your pain a little, at least it will help you bear it, I'm also going to prescribe you painkillers and Lexomil, take a quarter of a tablet in the morning and a quarter at night, I'm going to sign a one-week medical absence from school and we'll order some exams ASAP—he scribbles out his prescription, head down and sheepish over her file—you really needn't worry young lady, we're going to figure out what you have.

Dr. Fillet's day is ruined, spoiled by Ninon's case—he doesn't even want to listen to his patients' cardiac babbling with his stethoscope anymore.

Ninon leaves the office with bare arms, exhausted, she shivers, feels dirty, wonders when she'll be able to sleep, shower, get dressed without it being torture. On her way home, scared and distracted, she doesn't imagine for a second that the pain could go away on its own or even diminish, she thinks about the history homework she hasn't finished, the sweatshirt her mother promised to buy her, then about alcohol as a temporary solution, a possible hope while she waits for better, quickens her step to warm up and get back sooner, mutters to her mother that the doctor ordered her some tests, heads toward the kitchen, grabs the Smirnoff vodka from the freezer, takes one gulp then two straight from the bottle, the icy, burning liquid runs down her esophagus, relaxes her muscles, beats at her temples, she cautiously places the frost-covered bottle on her forearm, to see, to try, you never know, the pain is piercing, a slash to the skin.

Ninon can barely stand, the combined effects of emotion, the injection, and alcohol have finally got the best of her, of the pain and of her resistance, she lies down on her bed without even taking off her sneakers, arms extended above her, and sinks into a deep motionless sleep, a black hole, her arms fall heavily beside her body but Ninon sleeps, out like a light, finally immune to the unbearable inflammation of her skin—she starts awake an hour later, once again from the pain, from the burning contact of the sheet.

t's out of the question that she go to school, take a shower, get dressed; Ninon pulls on a pair of sweatpants, still in the tank top, which leaves her arms free, turns up the heat in her room and locks herself inside with a bottle of water and a box of cookies. She switches on her computer, starting at the beginning, with the simplest, the most obvious, she googles *skin*—she almost googled *arm* then decided that the problem was primarily dermal—and the first result directs her to a Wikipedia page, a litany of numbers, an arithmetic view of the human corporal envelope, an accumulation of data that isn't lacking in poetry:

The skin is the heaviest and largest organ in the human body (8.8 pounds and 6.56 m²), .2 cm thick on average but only .1 cm thick on the eyelids and .4 cm thick on the palms and soles of the feet. One square centimeter

*of skin contains 3 blood vessels, 10 hairs, 12 nerves, 15
sebaceous glands, 100 sweat glands, and 3 million cells.
The skin on the head represents 9% of the corporal surface,
each arm 9%, each leg 18%, the back and front of the
torso 18%, and the genitals and palms of the hands 1%.*

Learning all this—which she won't remember—
temporarily distracts Ninon from her misery, but learning
that the skin is composed of three overlapping layers of
tissue won't help her understand what's happening to her,
so she keeps looking, in search of a useful site, a forum
with some information, some leads. Ninon would like to
know more about the specific functions of these layers so
she can evaluate, for example, at what depth the pain lies, as
if by knowing this she could extract it—perhaps it's residing
solely in the epidermis, a simple malfunction of the nerve
cells responsible for touch, receptors that record the slightest vibrations and transmit them to the brain, but perhaps
it's deeper, and in fact Ninon has a hunch that the electrical
charges jolting her skin are radiating inward as well, toward
her flesh, muscles, skeleton.

When she tries to remember the pain, Ninon realizes
she's already forgotten it, pokes her arm with the tip of a
pen to bring it back; it hurts, the pain is definitely traveling
through the second layer of skin, she senses it diving into

the thick and fibrous connective tissue that is the dermis, then deeper still toward the hypodermis, now the pain is permeating that layer of insulating fat, spreading through the adipose tissue, sending nerves and glands into a panic, creeping into folds, wrinkles, pores, Ninon feels it moving, pokes the pen harder, fascinated by the intensity of the sensation, an ache that burrows in then rises to the surface, making the invisible fluff of her arms stand on end, and it's as though, during this flash of pain, she felt every strata of her skin distinctly, the stratum corneum, the stratum spinosum, the papillary layer, the reticular layer, as though each were detaching, floating weightlessly, and as though Ninon's mind were weaving through the interstices formed between these layers to appreciate every variation of pain, to decompose it as delicately as the wings of a fly.

She digs the pen nib in harder, jaws steeled, pulse pounding, and the pain is so great that she feels like the thin, flimsy envelope that is her skin has been reduced to its very flesh, raw, inverted, bloody, skin turned inside out like a glove—then she stops and it all recedes.

Ninon keeps looking, doesn't know what for exactly, but her computer screen is a buoy keeping her afloat, she types the word *skin* again and blinding pages of information stream by, she's been searching for three hours now, the internet is a forest of knowledge and skin leads to a clinical wilderness. She learns that over one thousand cutaneous disorders have been recorded (whereas our internal organs are only affected by five or six major pathologies) and these poetically named disorders—tuberculosis luposa, epithelioma, sarcomatosis, bullous dermatitis, and ichthyosis, which resembles a thick crust of dry earth or cracked ash—send her into welcome reveries, she loses herself on every page, in every disorder, dizziness growing with each new data, and discovers the story of the Viennese activist Rudolf Schwarzkogler who amputated his own flesh piece by piece until he died.

After four hours of searching, Ninon hasn't identified the disorder afflicting her, she's even lost sight of it a few times, forgetting the object of her quest, lingered for quite a while on epidermolysis bullosa, which is caused by a detachment of the epidermis from the dermis, then on irritant or allergic contact dermatitis, but in vain, nothing convinces her, nothing enlightens her, exhausted by this digital spelunking, she robotically clicks on a few more links, the bright pages blur, her eyelids droop, a final sentence at the top of a website she can't clearly identify grabs her attention: "problems with secondary skin formation lie deep in the unconscious," she doesn't see the connection, finally turns off her computer, wishes she could lie down but dreads the burning sensation of her sheets, takes off her tank top, and dozes topless sitting at her desk, arms crossed, wakes trembling and stiff half an hour later, it's nighttime, her mother's left for work, she doesn't see how she could possibly sleep, how to even go about it, an all-nighter is the answer, so she ventures into Paris arms bared; the thermometer hanging in the garden indicates forty-one degrees, she shivers, trots around the neighborhood a couple of times, wishes she were a large animal covered in hair, hide, or scales, warms up a little, keeps it up until daybreak, battles the onslaught of fatigue, she has to hang on, she has to get better, the nightmare has started, she chants this softly, nightmare, nightmare.

S kin: bark, thin rind covered by sensitive, vasomotor nerves, inhabited by glands continuously secreting odors, sweat, and sebum, a membrane that breathes, eliminates, perspires, produces hairs and nails, emits pheromones, keeps the body attached to the skeleton and muscles, ensures its verticality.

Skin: protector against external aggressions, a filter of contacts and influences, that captures and transmits stimulation coming from elsewhere, the vagaries of the physical world, and useful information.

Skin: with its complex, tactile, thermal, and algetic sensitivity, skin as a vital organ, the junction between the self and others, skin that speaks on our behalf, thin and vulnerable, supple and robust, skin that is all of that, and which Ninon explores again, in its digital form, the next day on the internet, and she wouldn't mind tearing hers off to be cast to sea or thrown to the dogs.

The pain settles in, establishes itself, after more fruitless searching, after two days and two nights of insomnia to be endured, after several silent meals with her mother—their relationship has abruptly deteriorated, nearly extinguished, Esther wants to talk to her daughter about what's erupted into their lives, think about what's next, present a united front, Ninon refuses for now, more stubborn than hostile—after rubbing a washcloth over her face, her legs, her stomach, after throwing on a clean tank top, it's time to go to the hospital, on foot, to undergo the prescribed tests, a half-hour walk in the biting cold because taking the metro is too risky, it's rush hour, the external world is now a threat, the slightest contact makes her flinch.

At the reception desk of Bichat Hospital, Ninon holds out the doctor's note, already full of hope, she's directed to a row of chairs bolted to the ground, she waits fifteen minutes before being summoned by a reassuring nurse with short eggplant-colored hair and fluid gestures who leads her to a cubicle enclosed by curtains—we'll start by taking your blood and then you'll go to radiology. The contact of the armrest, the tourniquet, and the cotton revives the pain, Ninon contains herself, the needle prick miraculously only provokes a light sting and the nurse doesn't notice anything—Ninon takes a certain pride in this, finds that she's vulnerable and lost, but also courageous and resolved. Soon the drawn blood will reveal the coded secrets of her organism, Ninon watches it travel from her vein to a test tube, a comforting sight, she hopes that they'll extract all the useful information within this warm, almost fluorescent red liquid, the truth about what's happening to her body— the blood will talk, that's for sure.

A few minutes later an orderly comes to guide her to another wing of this immense hospital, multiple buildings linked by paths along which patients stroll, cigarettes glued to lips parched by treatments, or clinging to their IV drips, in street clothes, sweatpants, or pajamas, more or less stooped over, more or less dragging their feet, more or less chalky complexions, seeking out the sun or avoiding it; Ninon reaches the medical imaging ward, linoleum corridor, swinging doors, milky-white fluorescent lighting, whiffs of ether tightening her chest.

She's asked to remove her clothing in a small changing room, to put on a hospital gown whose wide sleeves burn her with every touch, first for a lung X-ray whose utility she doesn't understand, but the young X-ray technician avoids her questions and advises her to ask the doctor who alone

JOY SORMAN

is authorized to answer her, then for a brain MRI that also strikes her as odd. A nurse injects her with a contrast agent, she feels the liquid flood into her veins, diffuse an unpleasant and heavy warmth throughout her body, then Ninon slides into the machine, a deafening noise begins, a mix of techno beats and stones in a washing machine, a magnetic bombardment that finally lulls her, distracts her from her pain and that's all she wants, to think about something else, be needed somewhere else, far, far from her body.

The young resident who meets her in a cubicle after the tests has blond, flowy hair, a strong handshake, and a confidence that bothers Ninon. Miss Moise, there is absolutely nothing wrong with you, he fires off with a smile, shall I show you the X-rays? Without waiting for her response, he places the films on a lit-up board and the sight of those gray coils, those troubling, somber masses, that spongy tissue, the sight of the depths of her body makes Ninon's stomach turn, it's as if she was seeing herself dead, dissected in black and white, she looks away. The images are completely normal; there's nothing to be worried about, I promise you, and the blood analyses are reassuring.

The disappointment is overwhelming, Ninon feels betrayed, furious that the machines are contradicting her version of things; she hadn't expected this, the doctor's dubious and nonchalant attitude, a diagnosis in the shape of nothing, the verdict given, an affront, that "nothing" violently ringing out, which, far from reassuring her, kindles her anxiety.

This young resident believes the discovery of the X-ray is the greatest invention in modern medicine and takes himself for the custodian of that marvel—project on the outside what's hiding on the inside, miraculously externalize the body, discover the pain lurking within without opening it up, penetrate the skin without force, plunge into the obscurity of the organs. This young resident wouldn't have liked to practice in the distant days of medicine, when they were content to merely imagine what was happening inside a sick person, when they thought that fever was caused by smoke in the head, when the only way to obtain a somewhat objective vision of a disease was to cut into the body at the risk of killing one's patient; this young resident is passionate and prone to abstraction—if he had his druthers he would tell Ninon the whole impressive history of radiology—and clumsy, and doesn't know what to do with the stubborn block that is Ninon in this moment: she hasn't moved from her seat and is staring at him, unblinking, full of rage.

You're saying there's nothing wrong with me, so why am I in pain? Maybe I have something that isn't visible in the

X-rays. Can you see everything with your machines? Ninon is on edge, her mood as combustible as her arms, she's been hypersensitive for a few days now, since this damn incomprehensible pain appeared on her skin, feels like she's under suspicion, accused of making things up; she tries to maintain eye contact but the resident has directed his attention back to her test results and scans rather than at Ninon's displeased face.

What I meant to say is there's likely nothing serious, nothing life-threatening, basically, to sum up, in the large majority of cases anything serious can be seen by the machines, but of course we need to figure out what's causing your pain.

And can't you give me medicine for it in the meanwhile? Ninon, persuaded she is the victim of the family curse but also determined to rid herself of it, was hoping for a clear diagnosis and a specific treatment, of being identified in the great encyclopedia of disease, was hoping that her condition would be named, that it had a scientific name to which there was a corresponding cure, a cure that would also have a name because the cure is always the acknowledgment of illness, its incarnation, because being sick means getting treatment—a sickness without a name isn't a disease, it's just shapeless suffering.

And so Ninon isn't going to leave this hospital until someone gives her a word, a beautiful and rare medical term, that will provide some initial relief, a word to throw in her mother's face, or place at her feet, it will depend on her mood, a word to hum or chant in the street on the way back, a word is the very least when it hurts this much.

This young resident knows—he was taught this early on in med school—that while medications heal, for patients they're also magical tokens, rituals, he knows that medication is the sacrament of faith in medicine, that patients are believers, and most importantly that the only way to get rid of this determined and short-tempered young patient, quite willful for her seventeen years, impressive to be honest, is to give her this sacrament; so he gives in, writes out a prescription for a painkiller in which he himself has little faith; he gives in to lessen Ninon's despair a little, to offer her at a minimum the word she's demanding, the name of a medication, until something better comes along, as the investigation continues: Compralgyl.

Ninon, somewhat reassured, goes to the pharmacy immediately, swallows a pill, sits outside in a park beneath a ray of light, counts pigeons then children, then blond children, then little girls, takes another pill forty-five minutes later, checks for improvement by regularly applying pressure to her arms with a pebble, but the pain doesn't slacken, the magic of the word—Compralgyl—is short-lived. Ninon is cold, leaves the park, grimly imagines the future, she's going to have to get dressed, shower, go back to school, maintain a connection with the rest of the world, control the pain, get used to it, and see another doctor.

Back home, Ninon takes an anti-anxiety pill, answers her friends' worried texts—nw I have the flu—then turns off her phone, slips on a short-sleeved T-shirt, the pain on her upper arms is intense but she sucks it up, settles on the couch, determined to kill some brain cells in front of the TV, to blanket her mind with images and sounds, to channel surf, floating and indecisive—a report on police corruption in Marseilles, a reality show, the twenty-four-hour news channel, is there any more vodka in the freezer?—and in the time it takes to make a heavy-handed arrest in a rough neighborhood, Ninon temporarily forgets the pain, erases it.

A little later she puts on a baggy shirt with long sleeves— it still burns—goes back to the couch for another hour of television, the time she deems necessary to tame the burning, to evaluate the beneficial effects of distraction on her pain, which, previously acute, has in fact become duller, pulsating, slightly diluted, and the tearing turns to throbbing: but Ninon's exhausted, can you live your whole life like this without throwing yourself out the window?

*

Esther comes home, cautiously sits beside her daughter, notes the long sleeves but doesn't comment, she's scared of Ninon now, of her reactions, doesn't dare touch her anymore, how are you? how did the tests go? Nothing came of it, they didn't see anything abnormal.

Good! a response Ninon meets with silence, getting up and heading to her bedroom. Esther Moise is no longer immune to guilt, now mixed with countless other emotions, a swamp of intertwined feelings that weaken and strengthen each other—anger against Ninon for refusing to share her pain and concern at seeing her distance herself, fascination at this new kind of affliction and worry that it will never be identified, vague satisfaction at recognizing the family mark and shame for inflicting it on her daughter, terror and confidence in the future—an emotional roller coaster that will end up isolating her too; soon two perfectly impenetrable walls of solitude under the same roof.

Ninon's locked herself in her room, she doesn't want to hear it. Her symptoms only appeared a few days ago and already the child who adored the family sagas has abruptly dissolved amid bitterness and hurt: although she immediately identified what was happening to her as something terrible, the sign of the promised genealogical tragedy—the possibility of a banal and fleeting inflammation isn't considered; this thing can only be serious, tragic—Ninon then decided to ignore her family history, to press mute, with the hunch that this ignorance would lead to salvation, that only will and discipline can break the curse, that it will resolve on its own; and Ninon doesn't see any paradox in that, simply believes that healing can't come from the origin of an affliction, that endemic and restored are contradictory notions.

This is why Ninon plans to keep her distance from Esther, and here the pain will help her, the pain will transport her, into a silent bubble, into isolation, where she'll have to struggle not to get trapped inside her own body, to escape this painful obsession threatening to take over, to exclude the rest of the world, absolutely everything that's not her—and in fact Ninon already doesn't want to think about anything besides her worthless, tormented skin.

O n her eighth birthday Ninon blew out a candle in the shape of a princess, ate two pieces of strawberry shortcake, and opened her gift, a magician's chest, then it was time for bed, the ritual, the story; for the occasion Esther Moise recounted a famous episode from the family narrative, one of its most spectacular cases, according to her own hierarchy, which always favors borderline nervous conditions: Celeste Quigne, born in the 1920s, afflicted by unexplainable fits of laughter.

The fits began when she was eight years old, Ninon's age, and only ended once puberty had passed. No one knows what triggered the first one, a joke perhaps, an exchange of looks that degenerated. It was just another day and, without warning, for no reason, the child burst into laughter, a sudden, inextinguishable exclamation, mixed with tears. It lasted several minutes then abruptly stopped. They asked Celeste what had made her laugh, she didn't know, she didn't feel particularly joyful, it had *slipped out, and now she felt exhausted; her eyes were ringed with purplish halos, her hands trembling, her heart racing, her mouth chalky, her throat on fire, her entire body still shaking.*

This was just the start of a long series: for ten years, every week, Celeste Quigne endured one or two attacks whose duration ranged from a few minutes to a few hours. These spells were accompanied by crying, fever, sometimes chaotic and violent gestures when her father attempted to restrain her; he feared that Celeste's nerves would eventually give out, imagining them taut, stretched to the max like elastic bands about to break and hit you smack in the face.

The rare moments of respite plunged the little girl into a state of anxiety and prostration—looking out for the next tremor— and science, as it often does, provided little comfort, no reliable explanation. Blood tests, saliva analyses, and spinal taps, particularly painful in an era when anesthesia techniques were still approximate, yielded nothing, they were unable to isolate either an infectious or psychological cause, it took several years before the affliction ended, perhaps as a result of a decisive hormonal spurt.

As an adult, Celeste Quigne was no longer subject to unexplainable fits—she regained the human faculty of parsimonious laughter, a sense of what was funny and farcical, going from faint smile to loud chuckle—she led a calm life, suffered no aftereffects, no lasting trauma, and never looked back at this dreadful episode, gave birth without epidurals to four boys and one girl, then died in her bed at eighty-six..

Ninon asked her mother what an epidural was, didn't really understand the answer, and fell asleep right away clutching a stuffed turtle to her stomach.

Ninon has an appointment with a dermatologist recommended by the young resident from the radiology department, an ageless woman, skin as white as rice powder, she seems a little fidgety but pleasant. The imposing red *Vidal*, the French dictionary of medications, reigns over a desk cluttered with papers and boxes of medicine, her gaze is metallic, two slits in lieu of eyes. Ninon explains her case in a now controlled voice, hands over the results of the analyses.

I don't even understand why they sent you to take these tests, except to reassure themselves that you don't have multiple sclerosis, the dermatologist shrugs, looks at Ninon kindly, maybe they should have examined your skin before peeking into your brain, everything can be seen on the skin you know, everything shows—she lifted an index finger in the air and Ninon's hope was revived—come on, young lady, I'm going to examine you.

Just like the radiologist believed his specialty to be the most beautiful and noblest one, the dermatologist believes that there is no practice more admirable then her own—pallor, redness, blotches, eczema, rosacea, erythema, pustules, the skin is the printed page of the body, the skin is where the depths emerge, countless diseases have a cutaneous manifestation and that's what's so fascinating, that indefectible alliance between the viscera and the epidermis.

Ninon gets undressed, lies down on an exam table, the imitation leather irritates the backs of her arms, the doctor applies fairly strong pressure, tries to delimit the affected area, does it hurt here? and here? here too? more or less? up to where? She examines the epidermis with a large lighted magnifying glass and asks Ninon to more specifically explain what she feels, to describe her sensations in minute detail: how exactly does it hurt?

When the pain appeared, Ninon instantly thought of it as a burn, has always expressed it as such, in this simple, fast, understandable way, but in reality "it burns" doesn't quite capture the fever on her skin's surface, "it burns" doesn't suffice.

Encouraged by the dermatologist, Ninon launches into a muddled litany, in search of the right word, says her arms are like a pile of embers consuming themselves without end, that the pain is the edge of a sharp blade, a bite, it's wasp stings, lashes of a whip, a cat scratch on a sunburn, she's looking but everything strikes her as approximate, and anyways Ninon has never climbed onto a pyre, has never been bitten by any animal, never been stung by more than one wasp at a time, never been stabbed or whipped till she bled—quite the odd process to imagine experiences you've never had to express another, intensely felt one—like an incision maybe, she adds, then finally gets fed up with this little game, the words fall wide of the mark, go in circles without capturing the "thing" (the pain) that remains shapeless, unarticulated, that clearly doesn't fit into any word, not even if you shove it—burn, burn, burn—or even a phrase, you could try, you could say, for example, a snake is coiling up along my arms, its poisoned tongue is licking my skin, leaving behind an acidic membrane, but that's not it, not entirely.

Words distort reality, they're impotent, poorly describe what Ninon is feeling, strike her as utterly banal in regards to what she views as an absolute, radically singular sensation; there's nothing more common than pain, nothing more widely shared, and nothing more ineffable, you can learn that at seventeen, she's sensed it since childhood.

Okay, so it hurts, but hurts how? The dermatologist keeps insisting, perhaps finding Ninon's indications confusing, but the pain has become a vague sensation, of varying and untranslatable intensity. Ninon, commanded to express what she feels, to express it with objectivity, has nothing clear to say, nothing as clear as the pain. Stretched out on the exam table, concentrating, she notices a spider spinning its web in the molding of the Hausmannian ceiling, is suddenly assailed by the terror of never recovering due to a lack of precision, a lack of vocabulary.

Ninon struggles to express her bodily sensations, the doctor struggles to interpret her words, tries her best to link them to known symptoms, one wonders how doctors and sick people manage to communicate, how doctors can understand their patients' pain and the circuits they take, how they manage to access them in one way or another.

Yet Ninon also has the strange impression that she's been more alive, sharpened, for a few days now, since her skin began to torment her without cease, as though the physical pain was invigorating her mind, as if this new bodily configuration had induced a new mental configuration, an acceleration of her intellectual faculties, quite simply she feels she's become more intelligent, perhaps an intelligence made denser, more expansive, more complex by time, age, life, as though her brain had been set alight along with her skin.

The dermatologist might tell her that this has nothing to do with her affliction but with adolescence, this phase of the brain's maturation coinciding with a bombardment of hormones, a great wave of cerebral plasticity during which neuron networks are refined by experiences and learning, carving increasingly complex and organized pathways. Disease or adolescence, little matter, Ninon feels whetted, crueler too, fully aware of herself—she sees herself as vulnerable, hypersensitive, but also lucid and perceptive.

She doesn't mention her family's medical history, the epileptics and maniacs, her sickly and lymphatic female ancestors, to the dermatologist either and stands by her decision: molded and kneaded like dough throughout her childhood, shaped by all the stories told, she can decide to interrupt the narrative, it's on her alone to quit the game, to break the pact. As a child, she had prepared herself to join this mad lineage, but now that it's happening, Ninon rebels, she wants to leave the ranks of the possessed, not to stand out, not to be unique, but on the contrary to melt into the anonymous and homogenous masses, to become an ordinary mortal—both ordinary and mortal—to be a patient like any other who goes to the doctor because she's in pain, to obtain a rational and scientific opinion about her case, however absurd it may be.

*

After examining Ninon, the dermatologist isn't so sure of herself anymore, has lost her striking confidence, she's also disconcerted by the absence of symptoms other than the pain Ninon so laboriously described, by the total invisibility of the claimed affliction; she considers two or three pathologies, not very likely, but she has to posit a few hypotheses and likewise provide Ninon with some scientific terms or obscure diagnoses—perhaps a mutation of the keratin genes that provoke lysis and the dissociation of keratinocytes at the slightest dermal friction, or more simply a cutaneous allergy, an atopic patient allergic to nickel or rubber for example.

She sends Ninon home with antihistamines, which won't have any effect, suggests she wait a few days to see if it goes away, or if other symptoms appear that might provide some leads, adds that she'll have to put up with the pain a while longer, and to continue taking the anti-anxiety pills, they can't hurt, and in fact they don't hurt, daze her a bit so that the pain becomes slightly more tolerable, creating a tiny margin of indifference to her condition, that's something at least, now that the dermatologist's powerlessness has left Ninon crushed anew.

t's not going away. One week's gone by, with no improvement or decline, and it's all the more persistent now that Ninon has decided to ignore the burning, to shower, to get dressed, now that she's thinking about going back to school even though the pain is constant, is starting to carve hollows into her face, her cheeks, under her eyes, at the corners of her mouth.

Ninon returns to the dermatologist, who hasn't forgotten this odd, and perhaps completely imagined, case, hasn't forgotten Ninon's perfectly normal skin free of any lesions, redness, suspicious marks, such youthful skin, so beautiful, pale, and elastic, she hasn't forgotten the awfully serious and sad young girl, she's thought about it, consulted colleagues, conducted research, skimmed books and articles, and this time triumphantly welcomes her patient and proffers a diagnosis, tells Ninon the news, the key to the riddle: dynamic tactile allodynia.

Which in reality isn't a pathology but a symptom resulting from a wound or injury, an imbalance in the nervous system, a neuropathic pain also referred to as cutaneous hyperesthesia, characterized by exaggerated sensitivity to touch, an explicable and disproportionately painful reaction caused by stimulus that shouldn't provoke discomfort, a sort of dermal rejection that stops anyone from accessing the afflicted party's skin.

To summarize, something that shouldn't hurt does, a gentle touch, a light caress on your arms becomes insufferable, but why the arms? it's a mystery, I don't know the answer. For that matter, the extent of your allodynia is atypical, normally it's confined to small areas of the skin.

Dynamic tactile allodynia, what a marvelous, beautiful trio of words! wonderfully pompous and complicated, three words when just one would have sufficed, three words that roll off the tongue, and with the diagnosis pronounced, Ninon could almost dance for joy, she's finally been deemed sick and therefore innocent, absolved of all suspicion, what a relief to know you have something rather than nothing.

Ninon undoubtedly believes that the worst is behind her, that her recovery is imminent thanks to these syllables pronounced out loud, *dynamic tactile allodynia*, a near alexandrine that's already keeping the pain at bay, an offering from doctor to patient, Ninon articulates the rhythmic and delightfully resonant words, they are the solution, because if the disease exists, brought out from the shadows, from clandestinity, pinned onto the big map of pathologies, it means she can be treated, describing a disease is the first step to overcoming it, name an affliction and you're on the path to defeating it.

The dermatologist explains to Ninon that the causes of allodynia are unknown, that it's a condition that affects the nerves and distorts the information being sent to the brain, that research hasn't yet identified the specific mechanism that causes this type of pain or narrowed down the exact neural networks responsible—we don't know if the nerve endings themselves are affected, but in any case, painkillers aren't effective, we need to find other, indirect, methods, to treat you, we could try tricyclic antidepressants, neuroleptics, certain anti-epilepsy drugs, or opiates. Ninon will test them all soon enough. But: is it serious?

It's not serious, it's mysterious, it's trying, it's rare, but you don't die from it, it's being researched, a little, it's not very profitable yet, but still, people are interested in it, kind of.

We'll begin with a precise evaluation of your pain and the extent of your skin's hyperalgesia, we'll run some tests. She scribbles on her notepad, that cryptic handwriting favored by doctors, undoubtedly so that their prescriptions resemble magical incantations, she looks at Ninon gently, with no hidden agenda.

Ninon walks back to the Rue des Dames slightly giddy, overtaken by alternating waves of despair and euphoria, unable to slow her thoughts, her heart constricting then swelling, cold and hot, she wakes up her mother asleep on the couch, three barely smoked cigarettes in the ashtray, a blanket on top of her, Mom, it's dynamic tactile allodynia, three words brandished in victory, and for the first time since everything began, Ninon smiles. Her mother sits up, concerned, dumbstruck—and?

Many of the doctors who studied the bizarre cases in Ninon Moise's family failed to heal them, sometimes even failed to simply identify them. Ninon, like her achromatopsia-afflicted mother, has been granted a lovely diagnosis, allodynia, but she won't settle for that; she wants to be treated, she intends on getting rid of the curse. And though a scientific designation may be the prerequisite for her plan, which is fully theoretical but imperative, to substitute disease for a bad lot, health for salvation, to write her own story, a question of biology rather than damnation, a story in which she's healed in the end without any after-effects, it won't be enough. Suffering in her turn from a strange affliction, Ninon is angry, reason fueling her rage, she intends, with formidable willpower, to convert genetic determinism to chance, intends, from now on, for her sickness to be the hydroponic variety, uprooted from the muddy, sterile earth in which her family has thrived for centuries, she wants to make the ever-menacing witches disappear, to escape her childhood, the age of fables, to join the world, the adult world, of reasoned experiences.

It's a conscious decision, to defy her own history, its presumptions and predilections, to go against her initial intuition, which prompted her, upon waking that January nineteenth, to think: I am cursed like all the others.

Well, they don't really know how to cure this condition yet, they need to find some treatment options, try a few things, but don't worry, Mom, I'm going to get better.

You don't look good, sweetheart.

While there's no specific treatment, there is the hope of containing the pain, of no longer being doomed to suffer as dictated by family tradition, by the fatalism taught by her mother—the sentence accepted, and not once through the centuries judged outrageous, you don't rebel against a curse, you bow down, you're a monster, a martyr, a saint, you're not like the rest.

Ninon has an appointment with a doctor who evaluates pain, a pain specialist. An office in the affluent neighborhoods of the sixteenth arrondissement, a waiting room with framed lithographs and sagging couches, a doctor extending his hand, this time he's old, a thick, drooping white mustache, round tortoiseshell glasses.

Ninon takes off her NYC sweatshirt, the cotton rubs against her skin and kindles the fire, she grimaces. We're going to measure the intensity and extent of your pain, and your skin's level of irritation.

The exam is performed using allodynography: a weight of fifteen grams is applied to several points in the affected area in order to precisely identify its limits, to map the allodynic zone, to evaluate the galvanic skin response.

Yet again Ninon lies down on an examining table, indicates where it hurts, her arms from shoulder to wrist, inside and outside, which is confirmed by the delicate placement of small, black, and cold iron weights, like those once used by grocers, hung from a nylon thread, which land like a lunar module on her body's flat surface, on the hazy geography of her painful skin, in an array of equally sensitive spots, her armpits, the curve of her shoulder, the crook of her elbow; and it's the same intensity everywhere, the same abrasive sensation, the test revives the dull nausea that is Ninon's constant companion, revives the lumps of pain, she concentrates on the doctor's mustache to avoid thinking about it.

We'll start with a quick stimulation around the affected area, then as I approach the primary zone the stimulation will slow, the weights will touch your skin for a two-second interval, followed by an eight-second break. The doctor asks Ninon to close her eyes, to say "there" when she senses contact; then he asks her to look at a horizontal line drawn on the opposite wall, it's an analog visual scale from 1 to 10, the left end indicates the absence of pain, the right the greatest pain imaginable, if I place the weights here, where would you stop on the line? On 7. And here? 7 again. 7, 7, 7.

Now the doctor sets Ninon up in a tiny windowless office adjoining the exam room—table, chair, lead pencil, glass of water: you're going to fill out a questionnaire, it's a little long but don't let that put you off, the idea is for you to characterize your pain as specifically as possible, to capture it as best you can, there are twenty categories to complete, each one suggests various words to qualify what you're experiencing: the first ten categories have to do with physical sensations, the following ten with feelings, you'll see, it'll become clearer as you answer the questions.

The point is to conduct a seismographic survey of Ninon's pain—her body is the ground, the disease an earthquake.

The door slams shut, Ninon spreads out the questionnaire sheets, drinks the water in one gulp, it's lukewarm and slightly chlorinated, she notices that the pencil has been recently sharpened.

Does your pain feel like: chills, burns, cuts, rips, stings, twinges, constrictions, spasms, quivers, punches, throbbing, itching, crushing, stretching, twisting, wrenching, tingling, pinching, pins and needles, numbness, tightness, heaviness, electrical shocks, hammer blows, knife stabs? Cross out any that do not apply.

Would you describe your pain as: uncomfortable, cumbersome, pervasive, radiating, suffocating, exhausting, tiring, oppressive, anxiety-provoking, insistent, agonizing, exasperating, infuriating, depressing, annoying, trying, suicidal, awful, intense, horrible, unbearable, nauseating, dizzying, cruel? Circle the applicable terms.

At first it strikes Ninon as a joke, one that's not funny, she's speechless before the mountain of words, far too tired to make the effort to appreciate this semantic fine-tuning, to distinguish the nuances in meaning; these words—though they're the very ones she lacked—won't shed more light on her condition, will only further confuse her sensations. Is the only way to master pain to name it little by little? To envelop a halo of pain in a halo of words? To make their respective outlines coincide?

Ninon starts to read, patiently, reads every word, reads them again, then aloud to evaluate their effect, all while poking her arm with the pencil tip, hoping for a magical reaction, a verbal miracle, but the pain remains stubborn, difficult, it won't be defeated by an army of words, the army falters, collapses against an armored wall. Ninon makes another attempt to concentrate on the exercise, wants to please the doctor, win him over, as though she needs to seduce him before he'll agree to treat her, she ends up circling a dozen words, including "twisting" and "insistent."

To these words she could have added noises, an assortment of moans and cries expelled by a broken and guttural voice, plus groans, teeth gnashing, joints cracking, nails squeaking on a blackboard, a knife being sharpened, a few sobs and silence—a rich physical and bestial language that has nothing to do with speech.

Later, as the allodynia continues to eat away at her, Ninon will keep looking for a way to express this erosive pain, not necessarily to others, to doctors, but simply for herself; she'll find a fitting language in music, dark, abrasive punk, pulsating hip-hop beats, deep electro pads, to express every level of her pain's intensity, which varies according to the assaults against her skin—clothes, water, brief contact in the metro, an accidental elbow, sheets—a burning that crescendos than decrescendos, deep or sharp, a cord plucked or grazed, a question of rhythm, of symphonic loops; and in the most intense moments, the most aggressive, she summons an entire orchestra, cymbals, snare, triangle and drum, a tuned violin, and the black keys of a piano.

✳

Later still she'll explore other avenues, again seeking formats that can encase her pain, images, translations, a framework that can contain the thing she still calls burning, for the sake of efficiency, simplicity, but that continues to surpass both her life and her words.

What out there resembles what I'm feeling and what I can't understand? she wonders. There's music, lots of it, painting sometimes—Francis Bacon's howling, bright red images discovered on the internet—and one night, as she's dozing off, lulled by the radio, a marine weather forecast in that enigmatic staccato language, a litany inaccessible to the uninitiated, to those who don't take to the sea, jerks her out of her daze—Ninon turns up the volume, intrigued by these odd words that seem to echo her pain perfectly, to resonate with the dark matter that has colonized her, an inexplicable coincidence: a low of 965 hectopascals at 340 nautical miles southwest of Iceland slowly filling in place, expected to reach 983 hectopascals tonight, a massive southward trough remains, pivoting southeast, a new low forming in that trough, expected to reach 995 hectopascals at 330 nautical miles northwest of Coruña at 11:00 UTC, then shift southeast, related ridge strengthening over Scandinavia then Western Europe tomorrow, southeasterly 7 or 8, breaking 8 or 9 this afternoon, dropping to 6 to 8 tonight, strong gusts, rough to very rough seas, localized high seas in the north, Sandette Lightship southeasterly 16 knots, visibility 29 nautical miles, continental high pressure, dominant airstream southeast sector, gale warning over the Hebrides, Viking, Utsire, Dogger, German, gales to heavy gales expected over Fisher, Thames, Ushant.

Soothed by a kind of verbal hallucination, Ninon melts into the music of sailors, into the voice of "Laurence" on Radio France and, who knows why, these obscure forecasts evoke for her every inch of her raw skin, the throbbing waves of pain, and even every moment of her day, from when she painfully wakens to when she falls asleep in exhaustion, and including the few periods of respite.

Ninon doesn't know what *Hebrides*, *Viking*, *Utsire*, *Dogger*, and *German* mean, they're places no doubt, or zones, but she renames the overrun parts of her body after them. Ninon doesn't understand anything but she can appreciate winds, swells, hollows forming in the sea, gales and tides, lows— she's desperately looking for signs, and Laurence's warm and firm voice speaks to her of her body in the storm, far better than all the doctors' questionnaires.

After the allodynography, which teaches her nothing more than what she already knew, meaning the exact extent of the allodynia—though the patient's experience has now been validated by science—the pain specialist has Ninon

JOY SORMAN

sit down, reviews the completed questionnaire, bob-
bing his head, takes out his prescription pad and scrawls
something—I'll start you on a series of painkillers, we'll
see how you react and go from there—then, settling deep
into his armchair, hands crossed over his stomach, as if to
stretch out the moment, perhaps Ninon arouses sympathy
in him, perhaps her sullen attitude amuses him or touches
him, perhaps he wants to distract this young girl struck by a
cruel fate: I'm going to tell you a story.

For a long time I treated a patient suffering from hypersensitivity in his fingertips, he couldn't touch anything,
couldn't grab anything, and not a single treatment brought
him relief, so he had the idea to grow his nails very, very
long, to protect his fingers, to seal off this small, hypersensitive part of his anatomy, to create a kind of hard armor.
Eventually, his nails grew so long that they began to curve
over, forming eagle talons twisting in on themselves. He
came to see me regularly to show me their growth, his
family and friends were increasingly bothered by his tough,
yellowing nails but he was proud of them, proud of coming
up with the idea but especially proud of his little eccen-
tricity, happy to stand out. He made his nerve pain, once a
considerable disability, a new part of his identity. His nails
continued to grow into long coils, he never trimmed them,
they become quite cumbersome, he would scratch himself

and others, but it amused him; and most importantly the tips of his fingers had disappeared and he was no longer in pain. Shall I walk you out?

Ninon, disconcerted by this strange account, looking for a hidden meaning, in terms of how it related to her—what could possibly grow on my skin as a means of protection?—let herself be silently guided to the office door, a final enigmatic smile, a handshake, I'll see you in a month.

Ninon, once again disappointed by the pronouncements of science, will interpret the story of the man with terribly long nails as a sign she won't get better, and that therefore she too needs to find a charade, a subterfuge, a prosthesis to keep on living.

She turns on the TV, flops onto the couch—painful friction, an imaginary arm swelling, on fire—Ninon clenches her fists in rage, bites the inside of her cheek, jumps up furiously, slams her head three times against the door, howling, slams it enough times that a small purplish bump forms, so that the pain in her arm is expulsed, so it migrates to her head, navigates through her body, from one spot to another, so that for one second the burning and pulsing is more intense on her aching forehead, it brings relief, satisfaction even; one pain distracts from the other. Ninon wishes she could pass out on command, for a little respite, she's afraid

that the pain, the intoxicating, dizzying pain, will drive her
mad in the end.

The specialist signed off on a medical leave of several weeks,
Ninon dutifully takes the newly prescribed painkillers, tests
one after the other, dozens of pills that have no effect, do
nothing but upset her stomach; she spends most of her time
shut up in her room reading everything she can get her
hands on—fortunately, Ninon loves books, a taste for fiction inherited from her mother no doubt, pocket classics,
Maupassant and Charlotte Brontë; Scandinavian crime
novels, Stieg Larsson and Camilla Läckberg—surfing the
internet, lethargically watching American TV shows—
Orange Is the New Black or *Game of Thrones*—but usually
the pain tires her out, she can no longer concentrate for very
long so she listens to music on her headphones, lots of deafening drum'n'bass, the female rapper Keny Arkana, and
floats apathetically for hours on dense blankets of sound.

Ninon rarely eats with her mother, would rather grab
food from the fridge while Esther tries to put on a brave
face, sometimes knocks at the door to ask if Ninon needs
anything, slides in a magazine, leaves a bar of chocolate
or a scented candle, a bereft mother who tells herself that
this—the silence, the distance—will pass, that her daughter
will come back to her, that these are the difficult moments

of adolescence, that they'll find a cure or that Ninon will eventually regain a normal life because this is the lot of all the women in their family, each of whom lived through the curse, faring better or worse, and in reality, not too poorly.

One evening when her daughter agrees to have dinner with her, Esther clumsily attempts to unspool their genealogical thread, as though to reassure her—you're not all alone, we always get through it, one way or another—but Ninon gets annoyed, upset, and even more so when her mother changes the subject, wants to talk about her job or a charming man she met at the end of a showing, a movie review in *Le Parisien*; Esther's cautious, excessively gentle voice fills Ninon with rage; she doesn't finish her salmon lasagna and leaves the table, she suddenly feels dizzy.

Ninon is depressed, has more and more trouble sleeping, loses her appetite, grows thin, pale, bad-tempered, the slightest irritation unleashes a storm—her bedroom door not properly closed, a DVD not in its case—her miserable mind taken prisoner by her painful skin, cloistered in her room, everything black and hopeless, Ninon can't imagine maintaining a relationship with her friends, who for that matter wouldn't recognize her—she keeps them at a distance with enigmatic texts about a benign but contagious disorder, absurdly claiming she's lost her voice to avoid answering the phone—barely says anything anymore, except a few muttered curses at every burning contact, every snap of pain that feeds her sadness, nourishes the ferocious beast thriving beneath her skin, and is beginning to take apart her life—the days go by, two months already.

Now there's a slightly different face in the mirror, one lined with anxiety, features drawn, veins protruding at her temples, she studies this face deformed by pain that has clearly settled in, no discussion, no downtime. The thin cotton shirt on her skin hurts, she hates how she looks, like she's wearing a carnival mask, soon it'll freeze in a permanent grimace. Lacking any other way to say it, all the objective ways to describe pain, the contrasting emotional ones, Ninon thinks: it hurts. She gives a faint smile, it occurs to her that life used to be simple and understated and that her effortless habits won't be effortless anymore, that it's crazy how easy things are when you're in good health, as though existence is abstract, an idea almost, just a word, and how it becomes terribly concrete when you're in pain, how thick and heavy it becomes, no longer that peaceful, instinctual stride, the wind at your back day after day, of no concern whatever, the peaceful river that flows inside you as naturally as the blood in your veins, a heart that beats and one foot in front of the other, the continuous experience of health and youth suddenly fractured, the supple and invisible thread of everyday life broken, Ninon feels like she's aged a century, expulsed from her youth and her body, a body betraying its own cause, a once perfect mechanism now a cloak of pain, her familiar, complicit body disappearing, ceding to a hostile, reticent, willful version, a body she no longer recognizes, it's a betrayal of life itself, its indifference flagrant, a blind bulldozer whose violent and disorganized movements awakened a demon, life going off the rails within her. Of course to live means to gradually diminish the very possibilities of life, but it's a little early for Ninon, it's a little early to lose the carefree, almost unconscious, habit of being perfectly alive.

Only the thoughts rolling around her head remain more or less intact, as if the pain had paralyzed everything except her brain, a miraculously preserved glade, Ninon can think clearly in spite of her dark mood, in spite of her anxiety that her affliction will take hold, that it will cover every inch of her skin, expand downward into her flesh, contaminate every organ, swell inside every recess of her body, and make it implode.

E *sther Moise, particularly scrupulous when it comes to relaying the family history, points out to her daughter early on that what is remarkable, and undoubtedly fascinating in terms of science, about their hereditary curse is that it evolves in accordance with the times, adapting to the circumstances—pathologies in keeping with their era, that correspond to the peculiarities of the century during which they thrive; therefore, no cases of leprosy or sorcery in the twentieth century, no woman exorcized, burnt at the stake, condemned by the Church.*

Ninon's genealogical tree is a Darwinian tree, a phylogenetic tree tracing both lines of descent and the evolution of living organisms, the transformations of their morphological characters over generations, the diversification of forms of life.

In ninth grade, the only biology class of any interest to Ninon was dedicated to the theory of evolution; she felt as if the class was talking about her, about her family, as if she was hearing her own story, the story of a common ancestor, of species, and of change. For once the teacher's words didn't sound nebulous or disembodied, they coincided with what her mother had always explained to her: things mutate.

And in the twentieth century, the century of her birth, things had mutated in a way that initially struck Ninon as disappointing and even dubious, as compared to her ancestors' incredible sagas, too prosaic no doubt for her imagination molded by the medieval curse that had struck Marie Lacaze. They had mutated, for example, in Brune Clamart, Esther Moise's cousin, who became addicted to drugs as a result of terrible back pain.

Brune Clamart's life was a succession of trials endured and freedoms yanked away.

After graduating from high school in the late 1970s, she went to Togo, became a fruit seller at the marché, hair down to her waist and as pale as her big watery eyes, eventually returned to France, worked door-to-door for an encyclopedia publisher, ditched it all on her twenty-first birthday to follow a guy who called himself Paulo and lived in a Roma camp in Montreuil. Brune moved into a trailer with him, renamed herself Cloud, on festive occasions she ate hedgehog cooked in an earthy crust or squirrel with an aftertaste of hazelnut, but the good life came to an end; Brune was struck in her turn, by an affliction that left the doctors perplexed, unable to identify its cause or even its name, and which attacked the cartilage between her vertebra, slowly eroding it, as though a tiny rodent had slipped into her spinal column and was nibbling a little more on it each day. Brune had to wear a corset, Paulo left her, the doctors grafted a piece of bone from her leg onto her spine, she was sent to convalesce in the Pyrenees—lying down in a plaster shell for three months while the graft took, then another three months to walk again.

At twenty-three, emerging from that hell but still suffering from constant backaches, Brune started shooting up to ease the pain, quickly reached two grams a day, became an addict, a dealer, and a consumer, and overdosed five times—it was a shit life, she stunk of sweat from morning till night, like having a permanent flu, and every day she needed a box of Neo-Codion, an opioid cough suppressant, just to get out of bed.

At the end of her rope, Brune decided she had to kick the drugs, so as not to kick the bucket, to isolate herself for a year on a farm in Le Crotoy, in the Bay of Somme, to go there without anything, without pills, in the beginning she drank a liter of Ricard and smoked two packs of cigarettes a day to hang on, was in terrible pain, after a month she felt a little better, better enough in any case to do some work in the house and a little gardening, in the end returned to Paris a revived woman, took a sewing course, and was hired by a men's tailor on the Rue de la Paix.

✳

Esther told her daughter this modern-day story in one sitting, when Ninon was ten, and once Brune Clamart had finally recovered. Like every time, the tale was ritualized, a new episode in the family saga at bedtime, recounted once night fell, in her small bed of forged iron, two pillows beneath her head, surrounded by stuffed animals. Ninon hadn't met Brune yet but would two years later, immediately liked this hardened woman with odd expressions—it's hot as balls today—and who talked without embarrassment about her years of addiction—at night I still dream that I'm shooting up and then I wake up because I feel nothing.

But it was the proximity more than anything that impressed Ninon, the possibility of touching Brune with her chubby finger, of sitting on her lap: her mother's cousin was tangible and immediate proof of the familial disgrace, its incarnation in the present day. What had been merely a succession of legendary figures became real with Brune, her body still bore the signs not of her affliction—her back had eventually left her in peace—but of its consequences: prominent veins, yellow discoloration of the eyes, gray teeth, the traces of cellular anarchy, of hereditary chaos.

One evening, Esther, never blameless, often suspect, places Kafka's *The Metamorphosis* at her daughter's bedroom door.

Ninon reads it that night and as expected, as imagined, is fascinated by this startling and cruel story, she sees herself in it: Kafka's hero, Gregor Samsa, is her companion in misery.

Gregor who, like Ninon, awakens transformed one morning with no signs presaging the catastrophe. Gregor who flat on his back discovers his bulging brown belly, his insect legs frenetically twitching before his eyes, Gregor ensnared in his new body, his new skin that has hardened into a shell, feeling a pain he's never felt before, strange itches, and his unrecognizable, bestial voice, metamorphosed as well, all speech rendered inaudible, any verbal exchanges with humans rendered impossible. Gregor who no longer truly recognizes his bedroom, a space reconfigured by the new body occupying it, soon to be a place of relegation but also of some tranquility, before it becomes his tomb—Ninon scans her room, no longer quite so familiar, a box that is both prison and refuge.

Just like Gregor, Ninon can no longer sleep on her right side, the position is too painful now, and like him, she's doomed to lie on her back like a corpse, reduced to similar nights of insomnia and endless rumination.

Gregor Samsa and Ninon Moise are living the same nightmare, everything turned upside down, both have been expulsed from the human world, they inspire fear, and disgust no doubt, love is henceforth impossible for Gregor and Ninon alike, and just as Gregor's legs secrete a sticky substance, Ninon's skin emits a mysterious and invisible poison.

Their mothers are the same as well, impotent, doomed to stand on the other side of the bedroom door, to lament in vain once all contact and dialogue have been broken, the force of maternal emotion is useless here, empathy and love won't save their children from the horror, together they collapse, misunderstood, solitary, trapped in bodies that ultimately represent their sole reality, folded in on themselves as the outside world dissolves. Ninon will reread several times the passage that describes the cockroach at his window, poor Gregor who struggled onto a chair to look out at the street, now a gloomy desert to his insect eyes.

But though Ninon's suffering echoes Gregor Samsa's, she refuses, as he so quickly does, to surrender; all hope of recovery vanishes from Gregor's mind, certainty of the irreversible takes hold, resignation and then acceptance of his new corporal envelope come quick, within a few days he operates his new body with ease, opens the door, climbs the walls and ceilings, creeps around, eats filth, the metamorphosis is complete, it's taken control of his life, now wholly occupies the place of the old Gregor.

Ninon's afraid of resignation—Gregor eventually allows himself to die to free his family from their burden, so they can begin to live again. Ninon's afraid of getting used to the cockroach state, to horror as a standard of existence, that the shock will cease to shock.

Later, after reading *The Metamorphosis* a second time, in search perhaps of the key to her recovery, after shutting the dog-eared, yellowing paperback, which she read at her desk, back straight and arms bare, Ninon drops onto her unmade bed, intends to get a little sleep. But her burning skin keeps her awake, irritable, she doesn't dare move for fear of reviving the pain that has now stabilized, she's tense, all she can think about is how her skin, which used to melt into peaceful slumber, is now bristling with invisible barbed wire, her skin's become a hallucination, she watches her arms again expecting to see them turn red or veined or blistered, and as she watches them she thinks back to Gregor Samsa and his cockroach exterior, and thinking about Gregor, other images come to mind, images from color movies with special effects, and imagining them she thinks—free association, train of thought—of the superhero films that her mother will never watch because what's the point in black and white?

She thinks of this because of Gregor, but also undoubtedly because of the superheroes' solitude, their hypersensitivity, and their metamorphoses, thinks of them perhaps because they are, like her, like Gregor, guinea pigs, more or less consenting objects of biological innovations and experiments on living beings, she thinks of them as a potential new family, imagines herself as a transformist superheroine—once you're given a new body, you have no choice but to find a new way of seeing yourself, you have to modify your self-image, and a superhero might just be the most fitting form for this unexpected state.

Ninon, immobilized in her bed, is a superheroine, albeit one without powers, but her body has been modified, distinguished from everyone else's; an ill-adapted, mutant heroine. Here is a superheroine whose field of perception has expanded, subject as well to modifications on the nerve and chemical levels, ten times, a hundred times, a thousand times more sensitive to the world's vibrations, sharpened by pain and suffering; Ninon imagines herself as a member of the X-Men, as the little sister of Wolverine with his heightened senses, or Cyclops shooting out waves of optic energy, or Angel with his healing blood, then thinks of Spiderman with his radioactive spider bite, imagines herself as his daughter rather than that of Esther Moise, herself the daughter, granddaughter, and great-granddaughter of degenerated women—and this reinvented lineage is a modest consolation that momentarily distracts her from her dark thoughts.

After one month of ineffective painkillers and severe depression, boxes of medication furiously tossed into the trash can and the beginnings of an ulcer, the pain specialist directs Ninon to an occupational therapist to start kinetic treatment of her allodynic symptoms. She doesn't know what an occupational therapist is, but the mere mention of the specialty reinvigorates her a little.

An occupational therapist deals with motor and neuropsychological disabilities, they're a teacher, a trainer really, they will retrain your body and its sensitivity level, how it interprets pain.

But what a strange concept, the training and guiding of pain, because for Ninon, like for all of us, there's nothing more indisputable than pain, you can't debate it, and the skin doesn't lie.

*

Yet the occupational therapist who sees Ninon in an office wallpapered in cork—mint green scrubs (pants and a collarless shirt whose V reveals short, curly hairs), thirty-something, athletic—starts by telling her that pain can be an error, at the least a deceptive sign, that you shouldn't always trust it.

He has her sit in an examining chair, opens a metallic cupboard, and removes a small case from which he extracts, as delicately as if he was handling a relic, a square of gray fur seven inches by seven inches: a rabbit skin.

Let me explain. This piece of fur is a tactile therapeutic agent. I'm going to treat you through remote tactile counter-stimulation, by rubbing your skin with this rabbit skin. This will allow you to progressively perceive a non-nociceptive stimulus, meaning non-painful, on a previously allodynic cutaneous surface. In plain English, I'm going to rub this rabbit skin against your skin, using small concentric movements around the affected area, gradually moving closer as our sessions continue, until I eventually reach the target zone, at which point you won't feel any more pain or discomfort. You will have healed.

Ninon wonders if she's allowed to laugh, if the occupational therapist isn't a bit much, the process seems completely ridiculous given how bad things are, should he really be taken seriously? How can a rabbit skin resolve such a massive physiological mystery? Could it succeed when everything else appears to have failed, and for that matter, if it was as simple as this scrap of fur, why didn't they start with that, before the blood tests, the scans, the ineffective pills, and the never-ending questionnaires?

But Ninon brushes off her bad mood, she's ready to try anything, to abandon herself in the arms of medicine, which are actually the arms of an octopus, a swarm of tentacles, she's open to every experience, every line of inquiry, Ninon has nothing to lose and no more stability—so a rabbit skin against her cursed skin, why not?

And what breed is your rabbit? A Vienna Blue, they're the best, I killed it myself, take a good look at this fur, note how thick, long, and lustrous it is, that color is slate blue, do you like rabbits? This domestic breed, which is originally from Austria, is particularly docile, it weighs between seven and eleven pounds, this one was rather big, one bullet between the eyes, and done.

Now she likes the guy, Ninon could very well fall in love with the occupational therapist slash prince charming if he heals her, if he liberates her, she could sleep with him, his skin and hers could touch, a miracle, a resurrection, love would once again be in her future, and she'd learn something new—and does it work with other animal skins? an otter? a mink?

Those skins would certainly feel softer, and who knows maybe they would work better, but I'm guessing they're too expensive for the insurance companies. What about a cat? a guinea pig?

I have to say that we picked the rabbit because it's a perfect blend of all the parameters: size, softness, cost, availability, reproductive capability, how easily it can be skinned—did you know that it's very easy to skin a rabbit, you give a hard yank and it comes off in one piece, you remove its little pajamas and then you can eat it with a nice *chasseur* sauce, or just a bit of mustard.

Shall we begin, Ninon? Show me exactly how far the painful area extends. She indicates her arms, her entire arms, from shoulder to wrist, inside and outside.

The occupational therapist is silent, surprised as well by the atypical, unprecedented even, extent of this allodynia.

I'm going to go around your arms, maneuver at the edges, get closer and closer to the line without ever crossing it, for now. Together we'll establish the zone we'll be working with, the zone to be counter-stimulated, the green zone, and an off-limits red zone, where the pain is, to be completely avoided. Actually, if you consent, I'm going to draw a map on your body with this marker, the ink will disappear in a few hours. The goal is to slowly expand the counter-stimulation zone millimeter by millimeter, this is the zone in which contact is perceived as neutral, comfortable, pleasant even. At every session we'll reevaluate this zone, we'll adapt and redefine it according to the regression, I hope, of your allodynia.

With a sure hand, the occupational therapist draws a line extending from her shoulder blades across the nape of her neck, then beneath her armpits, back over her collarbones, more prominent now that Ninon's lost her appetite and the ability to sleep, and down her torso. Then he circles her wrists, at the base of her palms—two lines that isolate her hands from the rest of her body. I'm going to start.

For fifteen minutes he delicately strokes her back, neck, hands and fingers, both sides of her chest, light and concentric movements, as though he were cleaning a superficial stain, delicately polishing the skin. At first the fur tickles, then it feels soft; Ninon's still worried that the occupational therapist will drift, venture beyond the line, to see, to test, or even that he will cross it accidentally, she stiffens, he reassures her. Ninon relaxes, thanks to a momentary reconciliation with her body, a surge of heat, she had forgotten that this battered body could be peaceful, hospitable, that it could still produce pleasant sensations. Her skin shivers, reddens beneath the therapist's careful touch, and her agitated mind calms too, her thoughts unwind, everything slows down.

So, how does it feel? nice? not nice? Don't be afraid if I get close to the edge of the red zone. Does it feel different? not at all?

Through what obscure imbalance is Ninon's skin painful on the shoulders but not the neck, on the forearms but not the wrists, by what mystery does the pain stop exactly at the borders drawn by the therapist, how is it possible that the frontiers of the allodynic territory are so precise and clean, without any muddled, porous, moving zones?

During our initial sessions, we'll stay in the green zone but the goal is to slowly widen that zone, to gain some ground on the red zone. And when it's time, I'll begin in that painful zone not with rubbing but with light strokes, momentary contact rather than sustained pressure, like a feather landing on your skin for a thousandth of a second, no longer, before lifting off. It'll be like quickly running your hand over a flame, you both touch the fire and you don't, you touch it but don't have time to get burned, the motion happens in a flash, the contact is fleeting. Does that sound okay to you? I'm going to touch you for less than a second with this piece of fur, you won't even have time to feel pain, it's a matter of precision and lightness.

A course of therapy that plays less with space—the surface of the body—than with time—minimal duration, pain that travels beneath the threshold of perception by traveling beneath the threshold of measurable time, time that can be grasped by the human mind.

You're going to touch me at the speed of light and I'll be healed?

While the therapist, in deep concentration, serious again, continues to stroke, rub, polish, Ninon, to feign assurance, to fill an awkward silence, decides to ask him about how touch functions.

The touch cells, which are located at the surface, are called Merkel cells, they're found in large quantities in the skin covering our lips, arms, faces, and especially the palms of our hands and the soles of our feet. They serve as sensory receptors, recording the slightest vibrations within the epidermis and transmitting them to the nerve endings. When you brush your finger against a wall for example, the contact creates vibrations that are recorded and transmitted to the brain.

Have Ninon's Merkel cells overly proliferated? Did they migrate en masse, collectively repatriated to her arms, deserting all the other regions in her body?

Or is Ninon lacking in the keratin that allows the skin to endure stretching, pressure, and friction, to resist assaults from the external world?

Perhaps her skin has lost its impermeability, its Gore-Tex quality, that prevents chemical substances from entering while allowing bodily fluids to leave?

After the session, Ninon gets dressed, the pain is still there when she puts on her clothes, which immediately erodes the little comfort and reassurance gained, but she tries to keep its memory intact. The therapist hands her the rabbit square used to treat her, folded up in a paper bag, urges Ninon to continue the exercise at home, to stimulate the green zone six to eight times a day, for approximately one minute—it's more important to do it often than for a long time, to be consistent, and diligent, it's not the duration that matters but the frequency. Ninon takes the wrinkled bag that contains the talisman with protective virtues, promises to begin that very night and to come back in ten days to evaluate her progress.

If we don't get good results with the rabbit skin, then we'll try vibrotactile counter-stimulation using a device called a Vibralgic, which generates transcutaneous vibrations, it's based on the same principle of stimulation, I place the device on the area to be treated and we retrain the skin little by little.

Tribology, the science of friction, which studies vibrations and other phenomena related to contact between material entities, won't heal Ninon. The technique of sensitivity reeducation via a rabbit skin will fail despite Ninon's diligence, and despite multiple Vibralgic sessions with the therapist—whose power of seduction will diminish at the same pace as her hope of being healed, week after week. The red zone won't diminish one centimeter, the frontier will remain impassible. Ninon will have to consider more radical solutions, see other doctors, try other treatments, keep looking because even if you get used to pain, a little—and getting used to it is a bad thing, a disheartening and disarming thing—its intensity won't weaken, nor will its ability to cause harm: fatigue, darkness, and solitude.

O ne chapter of the maternal family saga makes mention, as a footnote, of a handful of cases that are not pathological but criminal, in the sense that they appear in police reports. The unique thing about these episodes is that they involve men, and attest to a different kind of deviance. As though, upon contact with the male branch of the family, a biological vulnerability had zigzagged and transformed into a social vulnerability. At least that's the hypothesis formulated by Ninon's mother, who was determined never to refer to the family destiny as mere bad luck, a designation that would have allowed her, everyone, to place a little trust in the resigned materialism of fatality, but would surely have also meant forfeiting something—a family struck by bad luck doesn't benefit from the same prestige as one contaminated by a mysterious affliction and developing mutant chromosomes.

*

And so to Esther Moise's great delight, there was an ancestor in 1925 named Hubert Lamousse, owner of a brothel located at 18 Rue Pasquier in Paris, who was convicted for trafficking prostitutes to Latin America; then his fourteen-year-old son, nicknamed Blockhead, who was sent to La Petite Roquette prison a few months later for pickpocketing and acts of animal abuse—Blockhead and his street pals were in the habit of using slingshots in the Jardin des Plantes to poke out animals' eyes.

Thus the pair, Blockhead and his father, though they appeared to be in perfect health, introduced anarchy into their lives in another way, which one could judge to be more flamboyant or not.

This tale of disobedient men pleased young Ninon just as much as the accounts of raving women, and you know what, why not, thought the keen-minded child, that's the kind of quirk I'd rather inherit, a taste for delinquency—become Calamity Jane rather than watch your body malfunction, victim to yet another metabolic disruption.

When she hears this story for the first time, Ninon thinks that she'd have liked to be a boy but doesn't mention it, not wanting to upset her mother. And ultimately it's on that day, when she learns that the men of the family were touched by disgrace too, that she realizes the scope of the curse, that of being born a girl: hormonal chance, genetic injustice.

The pain, savage and relentless, has made its home, and since it's not going away, Ninon decides to put a halt to the succession of sick days, to leave the confinement of her room, to resume a normal life, at least in part, or a semblance, to return to something of the constancy of the existence she'd been leading until then, until disaster struck.

A normal life, she convinces herself, because it's normal to get sick when you're alive, in fact it's proof of life as much as its peril, and given that the sickness is lingering, burrowing its hole, spreading its strangeness, fragmenting her poor teenage body, given that her allodynia is a cunning entity trying to rob her of her autonomy, to eject her from her own body and take all the available space, she has no choice but to put up some resistance.

She decides to resumes her classes, as many as she can, only opting out of gym, and to coexist with the pain provoked by the many involuntary and daily contacts: the light touches that normally go unnoticed in a flurry of activity, the incessant, all the more noticeable now, knife blows; Ninon sucks it up, she grits her teeth, the enamel of which, under duress, is crumbling into invisible particles.

Ninon returns to school with a suitable doctor's note, written in vague and slightly anxiety-inducing terms, which attests to a condition that causes fatigue and requires certain modifications. She makes up complex neurological ailments to justify her absences and her tiredness, doesn't see how this allodynia business could be taken seriously, doesn't have the energy to explain, to confront sympathetic or confused faces, nor distressed or suspicious ones, the what's wrong with you?, the oh sweetie what a nightmare, and Ninon, crushed by exhaustion, can't imagine making the slightest extra effort—finding your words, back and forths, answering questions, thanking people for their concern.

Her grades go down but her teachers leave her alone, don't try to find out more about this student flagged as a unique case, though quiet and well behaved, and she's expected to graduate; Ninon still reads a lot, never goes out, focused on the effort required to attend class almost every day, she saves her strength, doesn't participate in conversations, can't hang out on a bench for hours on end with cans of beer and bags of chips, showing off and fooling around, so her friends retreat, she keeps them at a distance, without sadness because she's anesthetized, her emotional current interrupted, feelings shut off, everything's been turned off except her hypersensitive arms.

Her three best friends didn't give up easily, upset, offended even, by Ninon's strange and evasive behavior. They sent multiple concerned, insistent messages, came as a group to the Rue des Dames to ring her doorbell but no one opened, and finally summoned her to a coffee shop for an explanation—the table in the back reserved for the most serious moments of their friendship, the cappuccinos with whipped cream ordered on important occasions, prolonged eye contact, heads slightly tilted, an inquisitive tone, you've changed, we're worried about you Ninon, you're hiding something from us, is this about a guy? They insist, full of compassion and voracious curiosity, but are met with denials, cagey answers about her illness, then stubborn silence from Ninon, who loses patience—there's nothing you can do to help me, this is the way it is, just drop it—indifferent to her girlfriends' empathetic, suspicious, and then outraged attitudes, pushing away the affectionate hands authoritatively placed on her forearms, and finally leaves them there to speculate about the worst possible psychological scenarios and discuss their friend's arrogance and enduring strange behavior among themselves.

She's lost weight, dropping from 120 pounds to 105, and half an inch, her bones are more prominent, her long light brown hair pulled back in a bun has dulled, her hollowed cheeks form shadows on either side of her face, she has the puffy, drooping eyes of an insomniac, looks ten years older, ill at ease, sporting light shirts and baggy and shapeless sweaters, that don't weigh as heavy on her skin—and Ninon's learned not to feel the cold, wearing a simple linen top when it's barely fifty degrees out—a canvas bag hanging from her hand in lieu of her knapsack, hiding behind a hat and scarf, everything seems to be saying I no longer exist. Ninon keeps her eyes glued to the sidewalk, drags her feet, shoulders hunched, world-weary.

When she's with her mother, she makes an effort, tries to be more affable, more attentive, to exchange a few words, on the practical aspects of daily life—meals, laundry, TV shows—can't really tell anymore whether she's mad at her or not but notices an emotional desensitivity growing as her dermatological sensitivity rages, feels gripped by cold reason as her body goes mad.

One evening Ninon agrees to go see *Citizen Kane* again, at her mother's theater, and then, grudgingly, to dinner in a Chinese restaurant on the Rue des Écoles, and it goes badly; Esther, scattered, uncomfortable, laughs too hard at the waiter's bad jokes, sends a dish back to the kitchen, chats with an old theater regular, while Ninon struggles to hide her discomfort, then her embarrassment, doesn't touch her plate, plays with her phone—which has stopped being a communication tool but still allows her to remove herself from situations—and sinks into contemplation of the aquarium: phosphorescent anemones and clown fish.

Ninon doesn't want to be bothered anymore, doesn't want any more questions, she wants to live her life, her disrupted, solitary life, and Esther doesn't insist, taking refuge in the same opacity, the same tiptoeing around, the same game, blindness, the subject's closed, almost closed, increasingly closed, it barely exists when it should be at the center, Esther swallows her worries too in the end, along with her guilt, agitation, and rambling thoughts, stifles her vague curiosity, she suppresses her frustration at no longer being able to serenely write the family history, hoping that once things go back to normal—either Ninon recovers or she accepts her infirmity—she can get her daughter's account and add a chapter to the grimoire, finally go from the story of her ancestry to that of her progeny; because for Esther Moise, interrupting the transmission would be a failure. Resigned, helpless, she's counting more than ever on time doing its job, and while she waits continues her nocturnal projectionist life and jaunts in cafés open late, despite the constant sound of lapping water in the back of her mind, a black and swampy pond.

Ninon's existence is now split into two equivalent blocks, the first half dedicated to her life as a high school student, occupied by the performance that is studying and going to class, sequences during which she endeavors with great difficulty to keep her distance, isolating fragments of indifference, of disdain when possible, concentrating on what her teachers are saying, mastering her thoughts, which are drawn to the pain; the other half is dedicated to the search for relief, for healing, to the succession of appointments and varied therapies, to taming the wild animal inside her.

But all these medical attempts remain pointless, they have no effect, and with every new treatment, every new visit to an office that smells of chlorine and hydroalcoholic gel, sometimes of cold tobacco, a cat curled beneath the doctor's chair, floor wax, or new imitation leather, the same sadness returns: something rotten, falling to bits, is lurking in her insides and has decided not to come out, not to say its name, has refused to migrate elsewhere, to another victim, this something is striving to destroy her joie de vivre and Promethean insouciance of youth.

The list of doctors that Ninon sees as the weeks, and soon months, go by lengthens until it becomes a kind of surrealistic inventory, a collection of every possible specialty, from the most serious and focalized to the most experimental, a series of random therapeutic hypotheses and recognized treatments that nonetheless are ineffective on Ninon, a directory of dermatologists, neurologists, osteopaths, acupuncturists, physiotherapists, gastroenterologists, masseuses, mesotherapists, hypnotists, allergists, and homeopaths, the sheer quantity of whom eventually alarms the insurance company, which shares its suspicions with Ninon's mother by certified mail—a letter that remains unanswered since Esther Moise supports her daughter unconditionally in this medical saga.

There was the charlatan who suggested a skin graft from a pig, whose anatomical structure, he noted, is similar to that of humans.

There was the renowned, doe-eyed professor who discoursed with great kindness about the advantage of being sick: suffering from one disease protects against all others because you can't be sick with two diseases at the same time. We all have a pathological double, it manifests in various ways as you age, but it's always the same affliction, you can't avoid it, you can only delay it a little, diminish it, see it coming and soften the blow. Your allodynia is the messenger of your pathological double.

✳

There was the dermatologist receiving patients in a tiny room covered in mauve curtains and infused with the smell of incense, who maintained that sanguine temperaments were predisposed to erythematous afflictions, bilious temperaments to the formation of pustules, lymphatic temperaments to bullosa-type diseases, and nervous temperaments to dry rashes and prurigo.

In the end there wasn't much action, not much in the way of treatments, but lots of authoritative statements and alarming declarations, like the one made by the homeopath persuaded that individuals are always to blame for falling ill, ceding to the irresistible temptation to make themselves suffer. They wait for the right occasion to provoke the disease, wanting to test their resistance, to evaluate their body's resources. The pain is there, theoretical, hovering, waiting somewhere warm, somewhere protected, we provoke it, we excite it, and bam, it hatches; the war's on.

There were the many doctors who searched for hypothetical anomalies and imbalances everywhere in her body, ventured new diagnoses, attempted to find correlations between allodynia and other symptoms, other organs, to uncover links between her hyperesthesia and a possible cardiac condition, or unsuspected rheumatologic pathologies, secret liaisons between the skin on her arms and her joints, to deconstruct the ramifications of her anatomy, to reveal new pathways in the organism.

There was the neuro-gastroenterologist in a starched lab coat who announced that once again all this stems from the brain, not the overvalued brain in your head, but the one in your belly, underestimated despite its greater importance: the intestinal nervous system and its two hundred million neurons, which travel from the stomach to the mind. He advised Ninon to consume more lipids because they reduce feelings of sadness; certain nutrients cross through the intestinal wall, joining the flow of circulating blood, float up to the brain, penetrate and do their magic, acting on moods—eat fat, oil, butter, cheese, really give it a try.

He encouraged her to pay closer attention to her biological system, to listen more carefully to the information broadcast by the bottom half of her body, assured her that her skin and stomach were intrinsically connected, and that the nerve imbalance causing her allodynia was without a doubt situated in this soft, teeming, and central area.

There was the seemingly depressed endocrinologist who listened to Ninon at length then determined it was pointless to examine her: treating an affliction shouldn't always be systematic, sometimes it's not a good idea, certain diseases are in reality the body's defense mechanisms, they ward off other, more serious and more painful, diseases. We shouldn't attempt to fix your condition, we don't know what it's protecting you from.

There was also the skin biopsy: a small section measuring four millimeters around was removed with a trephine, a circular blade used for dermal excision, the sample was placed in a flask of formalin that was sent to the lab for analysis, and everything was normal—the beautiful elastic skin of a young woman.

There was the intrusive doctor whose forehead was covered with red patches, who gave off a vague cauliflower smell, who whispered his diagnosis in Ninon's ear, like a shameful secret: did you know that the vagina, the lips, and the anus are folds of skin, the entrances to mysterious little caves, crevices in the landscape, and not distinct organs as people often think? did you know that the skin isn't just an envelope covering the body, but that it's also a collection of orifices, that it opens itself up and invaginates?

He insisted that Ninon think about these orifices, about what they signify for her—danger perhaps, a place of intrusion, contamination, are you a virgin, young lady?

*

There was a series of bone, joint, and nerve manipulations, water physiotherapy in a public pool, fangotherapy—analgesic mud baths that proved to be as painful as aquatic ones—pain-relieving hypnosis, and Ninon even considered, on a day of deep despondency, resorting to a primitive lobotomy, or perhaps just electroshock therapy, to permanently eliminate this goddamn perception of pain, to eliminate even the slightest sensation that her two arms are on fire, to give her a beautiful illusion of amputation and transform her limbs into phantom ones.

Ninon thought up lots of far-fetched solutions, ways to outsmart her condition, ruses and feints, like maybe she could inoculate herself with another disease, a milder, less debilitating one with more bearable symptoms, which would take the place of her allodynia, because if you can't suffer from two diseases at the same time, one chases away the other, it's automatic. Ninon imagined an ever-present flu, a touch of diabetes, an ulcer, a true and beautiful disease that was recognizable and irrefutable. She could finally become a serious patient whereas now she's just a joke, deprived of any physical manifestations.

*

Then there was a break—too many thwarted hopes and broken medical promises. Weary of being a professional sick person, because being sick, playing sick, had, in the end, become a profession, a part-time occupation, performed methodically and diligently, Ninon checks out, ready to confront what might come if she opts for passivity, lets nature take its course, the wait-and-see approach of "this too shall pass."

Her life is still stuck in an in-between, a purgatory where she waits for redemption, for the resurrection of her body, or else a lasting condemnation to a hell whose flames are already burning her skin, a murky zone between school and her bedroom, her age uncertain, Ninon feels old as stone, calcified, shunted between the pain taking hold and the force of habit harnessing it, between exhaustion and a numbing vertigo, between cold and hot, mind drifting and lethargic, like a jellyfish, Ninon floats, the world is fuzzy, like cotton wool, and her gaze is both myopic and sharp, everything's slowed down, bogged down, like in those dreams where you want to scream but no sound comes out, where you want to run but your legs founder in cement— this is the state Ninon's in, a steadily growing feeling of unreality.

n the meantime, to hold on, to forget a little, to keep the burning at bay, solutions, compromises, distractions must be found. There's alcohol, always vodka in the freezer in the Moise household, there are fat joints that her mother buys for her in small quantities on her way back from the movie theater, and all this appeases Ninon for a while—sipping herself into inebriation, calmly getting stoned, safe in her bedroom, spacing out, a gentle escape from herself, occasional surges of pleasure, muscles relaxing, eyes half-shut, mouth chalky, Ninon lets go, a momentary miracle, her heart—shriveled from worry—swells, fibers stretch, ribs open and expand, a pink twilight haze blankets the back of her skull, Ninon becomes light as a feather, stiff as a board, finally gives herself over to perceptions other than those of her skin lacerated by invisible cuts, lets herself drift between her interlaced organs, the alcohol and the weed bring her up then down, her stomach, her heavy legs, her head tilted backwards, the skin on her face uncrinkling, her fingertips loosening, the small of her back slumping.

But these moments of respite and divagation always have a price, a malevolent side; a few hours later they provoke violent migraines and incessant nausea, which compound the pain and discomfort, and the hangover further accentuates the hypersensitivity of her skin, increases the voltage, rekindles the embers.

That's why Ninon only rarely indulges in these detours, just like she doesn't abuse the sleeping pills that plunge her into a desirable and continuous slumber, black oil and no dreams, but make waking difficult—she struggles to reach the surface, it takes hours to emerge from the quicksand, to get rid of the dead weight on her shoulders.

So that leaves music, less effective than alcohol or weed but with no side effects, no tradeoff, music as consolation, her refuge since the beginning, a poultice for her skin applied daily. Music, Ninon's language when she couldn't find her words, restored to its primitive, cathartic virtues, its power to possess, music as purge, a bleeding through which you drain away fever and poison.

Ninon closes the curtains in the middle of the day, locks the door, bare feet on the carpet, volume all the way, turns up the bass, it pulses in her chest, reconfigures her nerve circuits, creates new pathways, reroutes her pain, her anger, and often her tears.

Her phone, plugged into a speaker, plays Shaka Ponk, Eminem, DJ Zebra, Keny Arkana, Klanguage, The Weeknd, Psiko, and also "Diamonds" and all Rihanna's other hits. Ninon alternates throbbing loops and samples of rap, metal, and punk rock, American pop, no French music, no salsa or jazz, a little German opera, it needs to pack a wallop, make your head spin, syncopate, raise the tides, Ninon glues her ear to the speaker, the walls are vibrating, her room is a rocket about to take off, she implores the music to bore into her brain, she's out of breath, dancing spasmodically, a disconnected and expiatory choreography, please let this exhaust her, Ninon, fist raised, protests all alone in her room and demands reparation from the music.

For this musical antidote to be even more effective, concentrated, injected in high doses, Ninon would need live music.

She dreams of concert halls, of bars with acoustic shows in the backroom, of cramming into the first row, eyes closed, detecting through the thin veil of her eyelids a blinking halo of red and green, strobe lights flashing in rhythm with the drum and the thump-thump of her overjoyed heart, of feeling the humid warmth of packed-in bodies, screaming the singer's name, dripping with sweat, losing control, feeling herself carried along by the crowd, swaying and moshing, she imagines the walls oozing and the smell of mixing sweat, spilled beer, cigarette breath. On her bed, unable to sleep, she dreams like someone starved for a night out.

She decides to attempt it one evening, alone, in a large vaulted basement near the Bastille that plays electro until two a.m., but immediately regrets it: lost in the compact and raging mass of dancers, in the throes of unbearable burning provoked by the constant proximity of her arms to the crowd, prey to its sudden and uncontrollable movements, its unpredictable trajectories, Ninon is a pinball ricocheting against blazing bumpers, and even the spellbinding music has begun to hurt. She quickly retreats to the bar, which is packed too, with cocktail drinkers, tries unsuccessfully to order a vodka-caramel shot, in an inaudible voice, finally bursts into tears and runs out of the club, furious and ashamed, doomed to reenter her safety perimeter, her containment zone.

After the vodka, weed, and music, Ninon, still seeking distractions and ways to trick her body, finds a new way to calm, bury, or parasitize her suffering: hurt herself, elsewhere, systemize pain as recourse.

Methodically injure all the other parts of her bodies to extinguish the burning in her arms, flush out forgotten organs so they come to the forefront, make the pain circulate the way she wants, inflict it on herself as she laughs. She begins with a pocketknife, cutting her thighs, calves, stomach, visible incisions, then Ninon burns her finger pads over a candle flame, crushes them between the door and the frame, and since that doesn't suffice, she bangs her head against the wall, producing large bruises on her forehead, twists her limbs hard, and forces her body into unnatural positions until she cramps, this goes on for days, over and over.

This pain as theater eventually bores Ninon, offends her intelligence, reflects back a far-from-glorious image of a narcissistic teenager uncomfortable in her skin and seeking attention, in the end she finds herself grotesque, no longer likes herself in this role.

The thing is Ninon's lost all capacity for indulgence during this ordeal, she's far too exhausted to tolerate anything that strikes her as mediocre, starting with her masochistic performances. Her judgments have become hasty and lacking in nuance, she loathes her mother, her friends, the doctors, all her peers, including herself. Everything annoys her, the regurgitative commentary of a radio broadcaster, a harmless question from her mother about what's for dinner, a customer counting out her change at the bakery counter, a child singing in the street, and especially her own negative, suspicious thoughts, her own impatience, her never-ending bad mood—this is the terrible state in which Ninon has put herself after what's now been five months of pain.

And so Ninon, driven as much by the pain as by her short temper, resumes, it's never ending, the mad round of doctor visits.

She once again methodically and systematically explores the whole of the medical universe and its specialties, once again gathers all the opinions, in search of an explanation, a treatment, pills, or incantations, whatever, Ninon implores science to do its job of creating order in life, hers having been flipped upside down, ass over teakettle.

This new chapter of her medical saga leads her to an acupuncturist recommended by one of her mother's former lovers: a sort of Chinese druid or old sage from a kung fu movie, stringy hair and beard, slight hunch, inaudible and slow, he seems about a hundred years old, curled-up fingers with knotty joints, dry palms, and Ninon wonders if he can even hold the needles, place them without harming her body.

As usual she takes in her surroundings in a glance, could at this point compile an exhaustive catalog of medical offices, waiting rooms playing the same radio station, walls in drab colors, more or less imposing desks covered with papers and medical files or entirely lacking in clues, framed family photos or lucky charms, garish paintings, wood floors or seagrass carpeting, pivoting, reclining, ergonomic, or fake-leather armchairs, the latest Apple model, medical records or insurance information on the screen, a tomcat sleeping under a chair, or the smell of disinfectant.

The acupuncturist's office is particularly worn, the carpet frayed and stained, yellowing window drapes, chipped painting on the molding, the heat is turned up all the way, accentuating a strong smell of camphor. Ninon explains her case for the millionth time, the old sage seems to assent, makes a series of grunts in the midst of which float a few words—*skin, center, bone*.

The whole thing amuses Ninon, and in reality doctors are the only ones who can still distract her, keep her attention: beneath their gaze, their hands, their instruments, she takes form and consistency, decomposed and recomposed by the succession of pronouncements, put back together with each new piece of information, diagnosis by diagnosis, test by test, layer by layer, brick by brick. Even the successive failures, false hopes, and disillusionments, even the doctors deemed incompetent, unpleasant, or intrusive take their place in this grand operation—the medical reconstruction of Ninon Moise.

Far from displeasing her, the scientific objectification of her existence reassures Ninon, the world of medicine has her in its grip and she feels that's where she's meant to be, she likes being viewed as a collection of signs to be deciphered, reduced to a symptom, a corporal mechanism, she lends her body to science, her life to a biological reality that surpasses her, she submits unflinchingly to the rigor of tests and screenings, a docile object.

Despite the old Chinese sage's indistinct, garbled speech, Ninon understands it's time to undress: I'm going to place the needles along your spinal column because your vertebrae are like small skulls linked together, and the bone marrow is a garland of little brains.

Ninon lies down, the acupuncturist places eight thin metallic intradermal needles, eight dry and superficial pricks along her spine, so tiny they generate invisible stimulation, maintained beneath the pain threshold, impulses as delicate as a fly landing, then he covers the lower half of Ninon's body with a thin blanket and announces: twelve minutes like this young lady. Twelve minutes during which the needles will trigger the liberation of neuro-hormonal mediators, will waken skin cells that are so numerous that the subtlest stimulation can produce extraordinary sedative effects.

He adds, again in broken and muffled French: the skin isn't a coat, it's a central point, and blinks knowingly.

Acupuncture is a practice that, more than any other, takes the skin very seriously—the skin as a receptacle of science and toward which the organs converge; all hope is therefore permitted.

Ninon returns to the acupuncturist four times: two more traditional sessions then one session of ignipuncture with hot needles, and finally a session combining needles and plants—the druid places a small cone of burning-hot mugwort leaves a few millimeters away from the treatment zone to warm the skin.

Ninon remains hopelessly resistant to all treatments, all analyses, all hypotheses, and the failure of the most aggressive and the gentlest medical avenues alike, including acupuncture, reassures her that she is right to pursue less orthodox therapies, to test lesser known recourses, ones that are more unexpected, far-fetched some would say, to seek alternatives in the nooks and crannies of medicine—with the blessing of her mother, who likes nothing more than to venture out to the margins of what's reasonable, and signs, despite her modest projectionist's salary, every blank check her daughter demands.

A nature cure, a course of hyperoxygenation therapy in Switzerland, grabs Ninon's attention: breathe pure and crystalline air that has never been contaminated, purge everything impeding her, introduce her skin to the benefits of altitude; and if she doesn't get better, she'll at least get some rest.

It was while trawling the internet, robotically typing series of words into Google—including *heal*—to kill time, hoping perhaps for a miracle, that Ninon landed on the website of a clinic-hotel in the Vaud Alps. The homepage boasts a photo of snowy mountaintops and an introduction that mentions carbon-emptied blood, aerotherapy and oxygen therapy, the use of atmospheric chemistry to fight polyglobulia, and regenerative medicine, which promises to restore the body's equilibrium, eradicate imbalances and nerve disorders, and appease and reinvigorate; and Ninon, sensitive perhaps to the moral undertones of such a revitalizing endeavor, relishes the idea of a retreat far from the world and the nostalgic fantasy it evokes—a postcard of an interwar sanatorium, a row of lawn chairs on a teak wood patio facing Mont Blanc, sickly, multimillionaire patients or young tuberculosis-stricken wives convalescing, various forms of neurasthenia and pulmonary diseases, infusions of edelweiss and honey, novels with thick covers in arm's reach, large bay windows, and a dining room bathed in light.

Ninon wants to try; perhaps the simplest, most unexpected, most ridiculous experience will turn out to be the most effective. Ninon wants a change of scenery, to see something different, to leave her apartment and her mother, to cultivate her solitude. So Esther Moise dips into her savings account to cover the three thousand euros that the retreat costs.

On the train to Switzerland, Ninon recalls the doctor who suspected a touch phobia, wonders if you can suffer from a neurotic fear of contamination, and if far from the infested, diseased atmosphere of Paris she'll regain her health, if sheltered atop preserved and deserted mountain slopes her skin will find relief, delivered from danger and from toxins.

She's given a small bedroom with a view, Danish furniture in light wood, mint green walls, a private bathroom, slender nurses. Meals will be served in her room or the dining area, as she prefers; she'll have access to a multimedia room, a reading/game room, a solarium, a sauna; from among the activities offered, she chooses the sealskin hike with a mountain guide—she'll have to endure layers of clothing that will burn her skin but she's counting on the beautiful view and physical exertion to compensate for the pain—sessions of light therapy, and therapeutic body wraps ("packing" therapy), recommended for her in particular to soothe her allodynia.

The first two days of the course of treatment are dedicated to rest and fresh air, on which she gorges herself until her lungs are ready to burst. On the third day, Ninon, skeptical but anxious, goes to see the doctor tasked with "packing" her in a wet sheet.

The room is warm, dim lighting and a hardwood floor, Ninon is asked to undress behind a screen and then stand in the middle of the room, arms and legs spread slightly— completely naked, and without embarrassment, as the doctor looks her over.

Two orderlies appear, buckets in tow, silently move closer, and immediately begin to wrap Ninon in pieces of wet, cold cloth: first her legs, stomach, buttocks, chest, then her arms, her entire body except her head.

The feel of the wet strips on her arms violently rouses the pain, then the cold gradually takes over her body. Ninon has been transformed into a shivering mummy, still standing in the center of the room, nobody talks to her, nobody explains the point of the procedure—the orderlies have taken a few steps back—her teeth are chattering, she takes a deep breath, starts to panic, weakly asks for help, is quickly wrapped in a blanket, then they turn up the heat, they have Ninon lie down on a bed behind another screen, and they sit beside her, the two orderlies and the doctor: you need to stay in this position for forty-five minutes, it's important that you move as little as possible, feel free to express anything that pops into your head, the slightest sensation, pleasant or otherwise, but if it becomes truly unbearable don't wait to let us know. Ninon blinks okay, overwhelmed, trembling, glues her eyes to the ceiling, waits; the orderlies touch her at regular intervals, delicately place their hands on different parts of her body, Ninon is silent, tries to decelerate her anxiety, to repel this glacial, paralyzing feeling, even her bones feel frozen, about to break like crystal, she wishes she could cry, run away, but remains immobilized.

But after fifteen minutes the discomfort miraculously dissipates and slowly gives way to an unexpected, swelling sensation of well-being; Ninon is serene now, her arms anesthetized, her body temperature strikes her as ideal, and she spends the last half hour of the packing treatment relaxed, eyes closed, savoring the extraordinary feeling of power.

Once Ninon's gotten dressed, the doctor answers her invariably pressing questions; like at every consultation, she wants to understand, obtain as many explanations as she can, judge her chances of recovery: packing makes the patient feel like their body is enveloped twice over: first, a thermal envelope that's initially cold when we apply the damp strips, then warm due to the reactive vasodilation that occurs upon contact with cold; and second, a tactile envelope created by the tight, wet sheets sticking to the skin. Packing is often used to treat children experiencing psychotic episodes or blind and deaf children with whom only tactile communication is possible; this method offers them a safety blanket that, during the forty-five minutes of the treatment, replaces their pathological casing, which is in crisis. Once they're immobilized, surrounded, "packed," they finally calm down. We used this same procedure with you, we replaced the painful skin on your arms with a new skin, a double skin if you will—the modified temperature of your body and the sheets wrapped around you—healthy, virgin skin. Unfortunately symptoms only dissipate during the treatment itself, packing offers relief but it's not a cure.

This is a new disappointment for Ninon albeit one tempered by the thought of short-lived relief: in moments of acute pain and despair she can always seek out a "packer" in Paris who'll grant her forty-five minutes of respite.

She leisurely completes her stay—mountain walks with rich retirees and multilingual, tanned guides, light meals of steamed vegetables and white meat, reading on the terrace, interludes in the sauna and hammam to reap the soothing benefits of nudity, and another packing session—all without noticing any major changes in her body. She returns to Paris with mixed feelings, skin still on fire but rested by this high-altitude oxygen therapy, and for once her mother thinks she's looking better.

The family narrative makes mention of several dermatological conditions through the ages, including the case, circa 1840, of Bernadette Millot, a laundress suffering from an impressive and inexplicable form of lupus erythematosus that invaded the entirety of her body.

The story impressed young Ninon all the more because her mother had a piece of evidence in her possession: Bernadette's diagnosis record, obtained by searching the state welfare office archives and kept in the family binder, meticulously maintained by Esther Moise. Ninon was allowed to briefly admire the yellowing, crumbling relic; the document noted: "patient of lymphatic temperament, average constitution, twelve brothers and sisters, four of whom are still alive, erythematous body surface, pallid appearance, slightly scarred." Then a prescription; the doctor had recommended hop tea, cod liver oil, white precipitate *ointment, iron iodide syrup, gentian wine, and most importantly, sulfur baths.*

It was an opportune era for baths to take off—it had just been discovered that the skin breathes, that water favors respiration, that the body is stronger when it can fill with oxygen. Doctors were prescribing ablutions left and right, hygienists were encouraging baths, warm ones to remove dirt, cold ones to stimulate blood flow and galvanize the body, sulfur ones to treat dermal afflictions and rheumatisms.

Esther said that Bernadette's skin eventually healed but retained deep scars, and a few years later—because you see Ninon, it never ends, there's no respite, tragedy begets tragedy— her eldest daughter, Victorine, saw her own skin begin to disintegrate, as though she had been burned, until she started to resemble a skinned piglet.

Every day for months, inside a sterilized room, the little girl, twelve years old, also took baths, this time of bleach, which was intended to disinfect her body by then reduced to one enormous open wound. The doctors would peel away scraps of deteriorating skin one at a time, like fragments of wet parchment, then it took another twelve months for her body to rebuild its skin surface in its entirety.

This history of baths, of restorative and soothing water, continued, thirty years later, with Julie, Bernadette Millot's granddaughter, who was hastily diagnosed as hysterical—like countless women in her day who exhibited disagreeable behavior—when no one could explain her muscle cramps and episodes of muteness. This time, she was forced to take baths for ten to twelve hours a day—a cure for the desiccation of the nervous system. Back then it was thought that these baths would have the same effect as the removal of infected elements: pieces of diseased membranes, responsible for hysteria, would detach from the intestines, tongue, and esophagus, and be expulsed from the body.

Julie, who was treated in Tours, wasn't lucky enough to receive treatment at Paris's Pitié-Salpêtrière Hospital, under the care of Professor Charcot, the famous neurologist developing new therapies for women declared hysterical: magnetism, electrotherapy, and hypnosis. The doctors in Tours had in fact suggested sending the young girl to Paris, but Bernadette, like many of the mothers and grandmothers in this odd lineage, fiercely resisted medical advice, and in general distrusted orders given by men. They preferred to stick with the warmth of an affective, familial type of medicine, to balms of maternal kindness; they kept the sick women at home, tucked them in, monitored them, made them drink plant decoctions, invited family members to visit, coddled the invalids day and night, benevolently watching over them, and prayed.

This faith in the therapeutic virtues of family, when science so often disappointed, was also handed down through the centuries, transmitted from mother to daughter, helping to maintain suspicion toward doctors and a feeling of superiority far from conducive to the healing process. These women always balked a little before entrusting their sick daughters to the specialists, though they always gave in as the symptoms grew worse. They intended to handle all their problems within the family, and convinced themselves that parental love has unlimited powers, that outside the world is hostile.

After Switzerland there'll be a new salvo of endocrinologists, chiropractors, mesotherapists, naturopaths, and even gynecologists, of hypnosis and relaxation sessions, yoga classes, and a magnetizer. It's never-ending, addictive, a medical frenzy, Ninon runs around like a headless chicken, her efforts are fruitless, and it's as if the object (the pain) of her erratic quest has receded to the background; it hasn't disappeared, of course, the pain remains exhausting though somewhat eroded by force of habit—Ninon's used to it, more or less—but consulting doctors, every type of specialist, has become one of those inflationary experiences worthy in their own right.

If Ninon's pain were to disappear, she might not even notice, a hamster in her cage, too busy consulting, receiving new diagnoses, testing new methods, intensely scrutinizing the enigmatic faces of all those medical professionals. And far from weakening her, this mania, this obsession with doctor visits, is keeping her alive, keeping her rage intact.

Ninon gave up on graduating this year, a decision her mother noted without commentary, she turned eighteen, not that she cared, or wanted to celebrate her birthday—Esther still insisted on putting a present by her door, a pretty cashmere scarf—doesn't care about anything anymore except the impenetrable mystery that is her skin, her friends are long gone, Ninon is elsewhere, and her mother is nothing but a furtive shadow whose sole mission is to negotiate with the insurance company agents to convince them that her daughter's dizzying list of treatments is justified; that's all she can and wants to do.

Ninon continues the back-and-forths between her bedroom and doctor offices, a hypnotic oscillation, alternating between periods of calm and bursts of despair that erupt in massive waves then ebb, and sometimes, in a daze, she rocks in her chair like her mad ancestresses undoubtedly once did, droning, moaning—why, goddammit?

But Ninon's resources are inexhaustible, she's never short on ideas, impromptu urges, even if now they're circumscribed to the medical universe, she always gets back up, pulls herself together, driven by a relentless need to consult a professional, to track down the best specialist, the little-known treatment, and now, how could she not have thought of it before? Ninon wants to be hospitalized.

Really, that's what's missing from her impressive track record, her grand medical odyssey, and isn't it time to start over from the beginning? the exams and instruments (a check-up) to once again abandon herself to the technosphere, to the experts and scientists, for them all to assemble at her bedside, every specialty gathered in a single spot, every hypothesis back on the table, and to once again find a retreat, solitude, somewhere she will be taken care of—the sweetness of dependency. For Ninon, the hospital is no longer an anxiety-producing place, consecrated to tragedies and bad omens, but on the contrary, an incredibly desirable and protective place; the gleaming linoleum, dim lightning, and faint smell of disinfectant and reheated food will bring her relief.

The extraordinary medical network she's created over these last few months makes it easy for her to be rapidly admitted to Saint-Louis Hospital for a few days, in the internal medicine department.

At the hospital Ninon gleefully blends in with the other patients, melts into a mass of kindred souls, pathologies milling together, she strolls along the outside paths as if she's in a garden of disease planted with proliferating, pollinating species, immediately feels at home in this hushed environment, a biological stomping ground where glances meet, full of empathy and humility, and also submission.

Ninon gets noticed right away in the department, for her voluble interest in medical tests, her thirst to understand, her atypical symptoms, the abnormal extent of her allodynia, covering both arms entirely, they've never heard of such a thing, it's never been seen before, and that, that is intriguing.

✳

Ninon is alone in her room, a luxury, waiting on the adjustable bed, the gown tied at her neck just barely covering her, soon she'll be subjected to an interrogation about her medical history, her pain, her habits, all the questions she knows by heart and all the sterile responses that won't move the investigation forward.

Three men in white coats, on which are pinned badges with names that Ninon deciphers and tries to retain, surround the patient—a tableau vivant, movements frozen, mouths open and ready to speak, concerned looks—they're holding reassuring test results (no brain injury, zero anomalies) and one of them, the one Ninon identifies as the chief, older, belly protruding, lifts a corner of her paper gown, palpates and probes, for the umpteenth time in months, it's getting old, applies pressure to her skin, to the organs beneath her skin, listens, taps, manipulates her joints, tests her reflexes, impotent like all the others before Ninon's silent body, the invisible symptom resistant to the medical art of observation, seeing as there's nothing to observe, nothing from which to draw a conclusion, not a patch of red, not the shadow of a lump, not the hint of a deformation or deterioration that would guide a diagnosis, nothing to sink your teeth into, nothing observable and therefore nothing logical.

When confronted with Ninon's case, the doctors are always hopelessly deprived of their senses, their eyes, their eardrums, their fingers can't find anything, normal cardiac rhythm, ideal pulse, no fever, no palpitations, no cramps, no yellowing of the whites of the eyes, no bleeding, no tumors, no swelling, no ganglions, no shortness of breath or congestion, still no abnormal echoes in the thorax, no vibrations in the abdomen, no cracking in the bones, no rumblings in the stomach, an abyssal silence, nothing to bring back from the depths to the surface, an inscrutable surface, hopelessly opaque—it's always the same refrain.

The youngest of the three doctors, who may or may not be joking in this moment, suggests opening Ninon up, since every external and radiological exam has failed, to finally see what's going on in this body's black box, to peacefully rummage around her insides, to penetrate the mystery of this magnificent and extensive allodynia that has never been categorized in medical literature, to finally be done with this thing that's resisting; because, joking or not, the young resident doesn't like being resisted, he sees himself as a soldier of health hurling himself onto the patient's body as if onto a battlefield, onto Ninon the theater of operations, a complex landscape, surface worn by hollows and bumps, crevices and slopes, a terrain on which to deploy the forces, each doctor, each specialty representing an infantry corps.

The young resident is daydreaming, but it's what Ninon is imagining as well, a battlefield where they'll fight it out, and she feels like they're not fighting hard enough.

Like every other time, Ninon is in pain and the doctors don't find anything, not cause or relief. The hospital, that great war machine, leaves her by the wayside.

Before such defeat, to make up for it perhaps, and to get rid of Ninon, who is needlessly occupying a bed, they announce, twenty-four hours later, it's about time, their verdict of a functional disorder—disorders are labeled as functional when a condition appears to be neither serious nor severe and when no lesion, injury, or aftereffect has been found in the body. The affliction is therefore merely the expression of a fleeting and reversible physiological malfunction related to a moderate metabolic dysfunction; the young resident adds with a knowing air: conversion of emotional distress to somatic symptoms.

Which doesn't do much good for Ninon, who still experiences a horrible burning sensation upon the slightest contact with her arms. She understands that a functional disorder is a disorder that isn't treated, she hears that it's reversible, but when? how? and what do we do now? If something's malfunctioning, if I'm a machine on the blink, aren't you the mechanics trained to fix this kind of problem?

The frustrating thing about functional disorders is that they leave doctor and patient with nothing to do, and more often than not displeased, upset really, rather than reassured. The doctor can't heal, the patient isn't really sick. The doctor finds nothing, the patient is annoyed that they find nothing; Ninon certainly is, judging, as always, that she's not being taken seriously enough, because of her age perhaps. Bringing her mother to her doctor visits would have been preferable, more convincing no doubt, but Ninon won't break her own rule: always without my mother.

So they discharge her from the hospital, need to make room for a more serious patient, a more profitable patient—a nurse explains to Ninon that with the end of lump-sum funding, and the new per-service pricing, her case no longer corresponds to the institution's revenue goals—her bed has to go to someone who's truly sick, who's proven their worth, proven their pathology, their pain, whereas Ninon has nothing to give but her word, intoned a thousand times ad nauseam—it hurts here.

*S*omewhere in the archives of Saint-Louis Hospital are perhaps the medical files of the twin sisters Eve and Adèle,
Ninon's forebears, who were admitted there in the '60s: initially
deemed hysterical as well, after a diagnosis of encephalitis was
ruled out, repeatedly poked and prodded by the doctors in the
psychiatric department, then treated unsuccessfully with a new
compound, haloperidol, an antipsychotic intended to reduce tics
related to Tourette's syndrome.

Esther Moise made a point of including Eve and Adèle's case,
understood to be less tragic than the others, the way you'd tell a
funny story.

Eve and Adèle had always suffered from Gilles de la Tourette
syndrome: the older twin, preceding her sister on earth by a
few minutes, was more dramatically impacted, riddled with
tics beginning in early childhood, prone to cursing, whereas
the younger twin employed vulgar vocabulary more rarely but

often enough to find herself, like her sister, expelled from several schools, the victim of crass ignorance among the teaching body and the absence of effective treatments.

The syndrome intensified and diversified over the years and at adulthood took on a new form that affected Eve and Adèle equally: an uncontrollable penchant for clownish imitations, which made their outings into town, and ultimately any socialization, increasingly delicate and risky. Home-based dressmakers, they had moved into a modest house in Romainville, where they cohabited until their deaths, Adèle passing less than two weeks after Eve.

Safe in their burrstone house, their bodies remained at peace, but as soon as the sisters set foot outside they no longer belonged to them, as if possessed by the sight of the world in motion, turning into funhouse mirrors reflecting every passerby with whom Eve and Adèle crossed paths. Transformed into identical clowns, into cheeky apes, the pair would spontaneously reproduce the expressions and attitudes of those around them, accentuating their gaits, exaggerating their flaws and expressions—anyone hunched over, lame, cross-eyed, with deformed features, one foot dragging, or neck sunk into their shoulders was shamelessly mocked. Arm in arm, the twins would be spotted on the street, wriggling every which way, making faces under people's noses, seemingly delighted and insolent, out of control, but in reality distraught. Their Tourette's syndrome never left them, caused them quite a bit of trouble, a few strikes of a cane and count-less insults, the mere mention of which would prompt peals of laughter from Ninon, who didn't want to go to sleep—her little chubby feet kicking beneath the quilt, she would ask her mother to tell her the story again, the last time, promise, before turning off the light.

As time passes, as the medical visits accumulate, Ninon develops an erratic and ambivalent relationship with her doctors, swinging between blind trust and skepticism, anger and reverence. They remain authority figures, it's undeniable, that way she has of shaking their hands with gratitude and respect, of thanking them while emphasizing their title— thank you, Doctor, hello, Doctor, goodbye, Doctor—the simple joy of uttering that word, the golden ticket. But for all her docility, her affected politeness, Ninon isn't taken in, and her admiration for the medical profession has finally eroded; and though she often tries to soften up her doctors, to seduce them, this act of submission annoys her, she doesn't like this placid acquiescence to the superiority of science, to the arrogance of those who know, and sometimes Ninon finds herself rebelling against a doctor's haughty or tactless airs.

Still, it's inevitable, the mere sight of a white coat or an examining table rekindles her hope, a tiny spark of excitement in the back of her cerebral cortex.

But the hospital debacle proves to be fatal, this time leaving a permanent dent in her admittedly inconstant, long faltering confidence in medicine; it's one defeat too many, the ultimate disappointment, Ninon left the hospital in the same state of vulnerability and suffering in which she entered, and that betrayal is unbearable.

Ninon's done listening to doctors, for good, a promise she makes herself, curled up like a dormouse on her bed, it's over, I won't be fooled again, she watches the day fade through the window, there'll be no going back, no weakening of will, the pact is broken. Ninon feels she's been shortchanged, her sin an excess of loyalty to science, misled by the doctors, all of them without exception since the beginning, by those who know, by those who can, but who offered her nothing but a show of impotence and defeat.

Her great esteem for this power turns to hatred, Ninon angrily thinks back to their disingenuous facial expressions and coded language, their esoteric knowledge that now strikes her as an act of violence inflicted on the rest of humanity, meaning those outside of this privileged circle.

*

Ninon's rage, growing since her allodynia manifested, for almost a year now, a fury fed by fatigue, isolation, and incomprehension, changes direction like a flame in a storm, shifting against her doctors, against this medical corps officially tasked with the lives and deaths of individuals, of everything happening on the margins of these two realities. They stand there with their stethoscopes and white coats, ready to unsheathe a prescription pad, and we place our existence in their hands, when it's not at their feet.

Ninon takes stock of these months of doctor visits, and what emerges is a feeling of injustice, or, more prosaically, annoyance—pain has made her proud, compounding the sensitivity of her young age—and the disagreeable impression that for her physicians, her pain is just an irritating symptom, its manifestation dramatic but with no aura or prestige, that she's a pain in the ass who doesn't want to enter a medical textbook pigeonhole, that she's a millstone, the bad news you see coming from a mile away, that what she considers to be her disease, a true disease, has been treated like a minor clinical detail, a simple malfunction in her subjectivity, when the doctors should instead be thanking her for incarnating this splendid enigma served on a platter, a miracle of nature, because what could be more fascinating than a sick person in whom a disease bizarrely takes shape, adapting in singular

JOY SORMAN

ways, gaining nuance and intensity with zones of shadow
and light, in varied shades, what could be more stimulating
than unpredictable individuals, than unique cases that defy
the laws and categories of science?

Ninon ironically remembers the now distant day when she
learned she was suffering from allodynia, and the relief
that followed; restored by the grace of a name, a glorious
verdict, the hand of God on her head, she thought herself
saved, the name was supposed to trigger action, the source
from which truth would pour forth, it was supposed to shed
light on everything, be the solution to the lack of clarity
in her life. But now everything has changed, all is lost,
the name is a repellant, making things shrink and wither,
dissolving the complexity of her sensations and pain, it's
swallowed up Ninon, the temporary and unstable host in
which the pathology manifested before grabbing hold, later,
elsewhere, of someone else, continuing on its merry way,
because people come and go, but diseases remain. During
her bouts of pessimism and moodiness, Ninon Moise feels
like a toy, a ball, or a piece of meat between the soft paws of
tactile allodynia—the kind of monster that inhabits childhood fears.

Ninon, once again cloistered in her bedroom, a place of confinement and disorder, curtains drawn, a vanilla-scented candle, music in the background, computer in sleep mode, junk food, books scattered, begun but not finished, read in the middle or at the end, graphic novels by Peeters and Schuiten, a dog-eared copy of *Treasure Island* and some Amélie Nothomb, DVDs missing their cases— the Coen brothers, Pixar, and *Mission Impossible*—tries to think but about what? to make some decisions, but which ones? Several months have gone by like years.

Whenever she drank vodka, or smoked weed, lightly gliding a few inches above her body, Ninon, in an unpredictable burst of serenity and temerity, used to imagine her allodynia as an extraordinary saga undertaken by her body, an adventure of knowledge and sensitivity, her skin suffering majestically, her body a thousand times more receptive than all other bodies, she'd savor the uniqueness of her situation, not out of masochism but because the pain produced such acute self-awareness, a feeling or impression of self so replete that she reached a kind of grace. In these substance-fueled moments of artifice, Ninon would delight in the subtle perceptions produced by her pain and, pulling on a shirt or sweater, feeling its hot, abrasive trail across her skin, decompose every fragment of this suffering, isolating every grain, attaining a state of absolute tension, a fusion of body and mind, brain melted into her skin, dripping into her pores, a feeling of such unity that she imagined, semiconscious, that this exact sensation might be akin to pleasure in a way, to the sexual pleasure that had always been refused her, or at least delayed, all the more since all desire, even solitary, had eventually deserted her.

But when the effects of the alcohol and the joints faded, once she descended, crashing down the few inches separating her from herself, Ninon was no longer a sensory adventurer, but rather painfully nailed to her body like Christ on the cross, bound to her skin, her brain stuck, obsessing—a self-obsession that makes everything worse, transforms into exhaustion with herself, into dark ideas, a monomania that accentuates her pain. Then that treacly blend of body and mind struck her as an abomination, she felt incapable of forgetting about her skin, of letting her mind wander, of imagining possible sensations other than scarification and fire, desperately embroiled in this disaster zone of her body, as if isolated from the rest of her anatomy by deep trenches.

Once Ninon abandoned the bottles of Smirnoff and the marijuana, renounced the unproductive aid of the medical world, realized that time is doing nothing, all that remained was the strength of her will, that's what her mother, out of suggestions, said to her one day—you're not trying hard enough—oblivious to her cruelty and clumsiness, because you can't force willpower, it's not strong or weak, it's in your blood, your skin, your guts, it's the body that decides, dictates movement, makes it rain or shine, the rest follows, up there in your brain everything else follows, it receives instructions and does as its told.

To test her willpower, at the smallest level, Ninon tried to correct her by-now hunched-over silhouette: head low, shoulders drooping, arms held away from her chest, giving her an apish or cowboyish appearance. Facing the full-length mirror, she stood up straight, attempting to remain perfectly vertical, arms along her body, chin high, to restore her former bearing. She lasted less than a minute then slumped down, her shirt rubbing against her arms, once again steered by the waves of pain and fatigue dictating her body's shape and posture—just like waves of pleasure no doubt, she thought—drawing anatomical lines, throwing her limbs off balance, distributing strength from the top of her skull to the soles of her feet, accentuating certain elements, the curve of her back, while erasing others, bust shrunken, diverting the gaze and displacing the body's center of gravity—the arms have become the center.

If willpower proved powerless during such a simple exercise, how could she count on it to get better?

In reality, Ninon had plenty of time during these tough months to understand, in the flesh, skin-deep, that willpower is a ruse, a clay pigeon ready to shatter.

The resident had proffered a diagnosis: conversion of emotional distress to somatic symptoms. Ninon had heard him without retaining the information, letting it float and run aground in the back of her mind, then it came back to her all of a sudden, the sentence slithered into the forefront, illuminating what she knew without ever formulating it, articulating it—something in her life was wrong and expressing itself through this allodynic pain. The resident had added: all diseases are biopsychic.

A nerve disease perhaps, since her family had produced several of them over the centuries, since cases of mental disorders were recurrent in their history, a litany of psychological pains, of brain ailments wrapped inside the body, and vice versa.

✳

Of course many doctors had suggested this, more or less directly, had steered Ninon toward a psychiatrist, or, for the more timorous among them, a psychologist, had encouraged her to explore this avenue, this last resort, once all the resources dealing with the body's physiological mechanics had been exhausted, since the mystery only continued to deepen and since, in that same ascendant motion, the troubling shadow of the psyche was growing.

At this stage of pain and fatigue, and the resulting depression, the time has undoubtedly come to resign herself, or to be reasonable, it depends, the time has come to swallow her pride and her preconceptions, and here once again it's a matter of medicine, the medicine of the mind, of the spongy matter from which it's formed, the time has come, when there's no other alternative, to acknowledge disruptions to one's metabolic systems, and to go see a shrink.

For a long time Ninon feared and rejected a verdict of psychosomatic pain, a diagnosis that didn't do her justice, her outsides were on fire, and so it was from the outside that she wanted to be treated, considered.

For a long time she refused to mention her family history, rejecting a narrative judged as indulgent as it was deliberately opaque, brushing aside the idea of inevitable transmission, the evidence of her lineage, an unbudging reproductive chain; all she wanted was to identify the reasons for her pain elsewhere, in the air we breathe, the electromagnetic waves constantly bombarding us, the endocrine disruptors that infest our lives, food, pollution, the sun, the concrete jungle, anything you like on the chance that these elements were residing within her white blood cells, enzymes, spinal cord, or amino acids. Ninon's pain had sparked a fantasy of a body without a mind, a dream of matter with no soul, a desire to be nothing more than an assemblage of flesh, nerves, and bone, because only flesh, the source of both degeneration and salvation, is worthy of trust, can be effectively manipulated by surgical instruments, whereas dark thoughts flee scalpels and X-rays. Ninon has enmeshed herself inside this certainty: flesh is the only possible site of intervention. This is what's germinating inside the head of an eighteen-year-old girl in enough pain to drive a person mad, and who dreams of self-engenderment.

And dreaming as she is of spontaneous generation, one imagines that Ninon will be reticent to address the inevitable questions: family, forebears, heritage.

And yet she decides to do just that—the resident's verdict, somatic conversion of emotional distress, brought a whole swarm of similar expressions to the surface, heard for months, uttered by more or less sympathetic mouths, and immediately dismissed, forgotten, I'll think about it later, what's the point.

And the what's the point becomes a why not, becomes curiosity as much as it does facing the facts, a following of orders and of recommendations, becomes one more stage in what Ninon views as a long voyage, an internal speleology. Let's dig into the layers of my psyche, see what we can find in terms of explanations and perhaps relief.

The family then, finally: father (unknown and who in Ninon's eyes has the merit of having passed down nothing to her, no name, no disease, no advice), mother, ancestresses, every eldest daughter since the Middle Ages, whom Esther has recorded without fail, reproducing in minute detail her genealogical tree with its countless diseased and twisted branches in a leather-bound notebook that she intends to leave to her daughter—a notebook as heavy as a spell book, a heritage as crushing as five centuries of kinship, a multi-layered history in the rock of time.

Esther's obsessive perseverance is precisely what allowed her to reconstruct the entire family narrative, for even though pseudo-official accounts of the majority of cases were transmitted from generation to generation, thanks to a preserved oral culture and some letters and handwritten notes, she's dedicated a great deal of her free time to this endeavor, visiting the archives of several cities, soliciting genealogists, spending hours on the internet looking for clues to fill in the holes of the genealogical story; and the reason she found everything, that the thread of time was never broken, is that none of her ancestors ever ventured outside of France, to start a new life, to break away, if only to get married farther afield; there were many senseless voyages and divagations but these were strictly internal, confined to craniums and viscera.

Esther and Ninon Moise's family is a French family that tumbled through the ages without ever leaving its motherland or even mixing in one way or another, a line of women who always engender other women with the same men, the local men, the Lacazes, the Millots, the Tendrons, the Quignes, the Lamousses, names that come to ring in the adult Ninon's ears like a repetitious, sclerotic tune—endemic purity, entrenchment, incurable immobility that she will one day suspect is the origin of the pathological disorder, the merited degeneration, the announced catastrophe, the explanation for this unnamable affliction that has been falling like dominos for five hundred years.

Ninon knows this genealogical tree well, as a child she would consult it weekly, whenever Esther revealed a new case, shared a new episode of the family saga, added a branch to the thick foliage.

Now she's rather inclined to uproot this oak with fossilized bark, to replant it upside down, in another garden, or to repot it in a greenhouse, dare to take cuttings, make grafts, as many genetic manipulations as possible to revive the degenerate branches, or else chop the whole thing down, make a pile, and burn it.

Does seeing a shrink equate to, on the contrary, dancing around the tree, scratching her initials into its trunk, adding fertilizer, and watering it abundantly?

The psychiatrist is a woman, recommended by the residents at Saint-Louis for her work on the skin and self-awareness. Dr. Kilfe is in her fifties: mohair sweater, short, thick hair, large gold hoop earrings, a small cozy office furnished with dark wood and layered Afghan rugs, decorated with framed paint miniatures and plant engravings. Ninon first notices a Lampe Berger lamp and a pack of tissues on the small side table beside the couch, then the tawny leather bench—intimidating and menacing—on which she won't lie down, it's undoubtedly premature at eighteen years old; have a seat, Ninon. The psychiatrist isn't wearing a white coat, doesn't take Ninon's blood pressure, doesn't check her reflexes, but her name is still preceded by the reassuring title of doctor, which, in spite of everything, in spite of Ninon, continues to have an effect, to spread its scent of authority.

*

The first session is a failure, not from a scientific point of view but from Ninon's, who remains mute, regrets coming, is ultimately annoyed to find herself here, amid this perfect, utterly predictable decor—just the right blend of primness and non-Western accents—discomfited by Dr. Kilfe's professional and attentive silence—she has plenty of time, thirty-five minutes, in fact, which costs ninety euros. Ninon doesn't know where or when to begin, with the past or the present? fears sounding mechanical or trite or vague, starts sentences with a husky voice and doesn't finish them, looks elsewhere, at a skylight that reveals the treetops, she twitches in her chair, vainly waits for Dr. Kilfe to note her signs of impatience, to say something, at least make a sound, a head motion, but nothing apart from a Lacanian version of a Mona Lisa smile.

And yet at the end of the thirty-five-minute session, Ninon promises to come back, caught off guard by Dr. Kilfe's question, a clear, raised voice: see you next week?

Encouraged by her mother, who sees this psychotherapy as, if not the debut of Ninon's recovery, then that of reconciliation, reintegration into the lineage—and psychoanalysis in general as a precious ally for her project of cementing the family genealogy— this time Ninon's slid a flask into her bag, takes three sips of vodka before going up, bites into a mint lozenge and sits down, resolved, cheeks on fire, across from Dr. Kilfe.

Psychotherapy might not be such a bad occupation for her brain overstimulated by solitude and obsession, and made pliable by experience and introspection. Here, like elsewhere, in other offices, across from other doctors, it's a question of playing the game, scrupulously following the stages of a protocol, accepting and respecting the plan, and evaluating its effects.

Ninon will finally let out a long, rambling thread of a sentence, the verbal mechanism in her brain warming up as the weeks go by, propelled by its own momentum, swept along by ball bearings: though she begins by voicing outrage over the lack of any analgesic solutions to her pain, not a single painkiller, not a single anesthetizing cream to give me some relief, she rapidly moves on, at the slightest encouragement from Dr. Kilfe, to her female forebears, their suffering to be precise, what they must have gone through in an era when doctors barely knew how to evaluate it.

The psychiatrist wonders whether their pain was more bearable in those times of religious fervor, less scandalous because it was expiatory, heightened by a moral recompense that made up for the absence of efficient remedies, whether they suffered like martyrs, like good Catholics, in the certainty of salvation to come, perhaps even with enthusiasm and devotion. Ninon plays along, grandiosely blames her own hopeless skepticism, says she'd gladly agree to be inoculated by faith if it existed in the form of a miraculous poison—that's all I'm asking for, for my pain to be sublimated by belief, my complaints elevated, for this whole thing to finally be given meaning, as irrational as it might be, because it looks like reason isn't cutting it.

But at the next session, still unwinding her mad spool of words, she gets worked up, just as theatrically, about the distortions of religion and the misguidedness of her sanctimonious forebears, announces that she'd rather abandon herself to the messiness of chance than to piety as consolation. At this moment, Dr. Kilfe makes a mental note that Ninon has come here seeking another form of sublimation, a system of meaning, a system of belief, albeit a secular one, now that she can't bear the thought of allowing what the doctor has often referred to in her articles for the *Revue française de psychanalyse* as a "garden of weeds" to flourish inside of her.

In the course of their sessions Ninon returns repeatedly to her pain and fatigue, to her growing misanthropy, which suits her, she says, to the high school now far behind her, the abandoned friends, to her mother who awaited and dreaded her daughter's affliction as much as she desired it, to the stories meticulously recorded and shared one by one, injected throughout her childhood, a patient endeavor of mithridatism, and of course, not without pride, to all the doctors consulted, the panoply of specialties, the treatments tested, her investment of body and soul, the exams to which she docilely submitted, frightened and intoxicated.

And after one month Dr. Kilfe finally ventures a few hypotheses, in a voice whose affability rings false to Ninon's ears, like condescension maybe: that she's most likely given up on any expertise on or control of her condition, that she was wrong to place total faith in medicine, to absolve herself of all responsibility in the matter, and also that she appears to have confused sense and meaning—it's not because your pain makes no sense that it doesn't have meaning; approaches that Ninon takes in for now without reacting, indifferent, disappointed to be honest, and which she allows to drift away as she waits for better.

But the main reason the doctors at Saint-Louis handed Ninon off to Dr. Kilfe was because the psychiatrist had studied, in the '80s, under the psychoanalyst Didier Anzieu, a professor of psychology in Nanterre and the author of a seminal work, *The Skin-Ego*, whose powerful and poetic thesis proved to be as fertile for science as for the imagination: the subject is contained within their skin. The book, lauded upon publication, became a classic and remains highly influential, in particular on Dr. Kilfe, who consults it regularly; practice psychiatry as incarnated by an organ, analyze impulses based on one region of the body, such is the mission Dr. Kilfe has adopted; and why the skin, doctor?

Quite simply because the ectoderm, the outer layer of the embryo, is the neurological source shared by skin and brain, because the two can never be separated; because the skin secretes the same substances as neurons, because it's a peripheral brain, the sensor that receives information, which is transmitted to the primary brain, for decoding and analysis, while the gray matter, the cortex, is itself made of skin, which covers the white substance. Therefore the skin and the mind are forever joined.

After the first month, a phase during which the feline psychiatrist lies in wait, observing, Dr. Kilfe opts for more loquacity, laying out the different aspects of the argument behind *The Skin-Ego*, and Ninon is fascinated by this diversion, far more stimulating than all the speculations about her responsibility, her relationship to doctors or to her family, now imagining herself in terms of this seductive philosophy.

It all begins with the image of the skin as an envelope, bark, a sack—you are a sack of skin that contains the body and its moods, keeps impulses and humors on the inside, otherwise they would leak everywhere, and blood would gush onto Dr. Kilfe's Afghan rugs, and your lungs and intestines would roll along the ground.

The reason people with serious burns die is that they're actually no longer watertight, they ooze out and spread; they are emptied. We are sacks of skin, gourds that maintain and unify all that we are made of—bones, organs, blood, brain and therefore psyche.

I am a body above all else, solemnly repeats Dr. Kilfe, I am a body above all else, and nothing pleases Ninon more than this affirmation, I am skin above all else, adds the psychiatrist, I am made of all the sensations that emerge on the surface of the body, the surface of the consciousness is homothetic to that of the body, they have the same surface area, the same reach, the mind isn't buried in the folds and twists of the brain, it appears on the surface, sensitive to wind and sun, to caresses and blows.

Ninon, you're a sack of skin but you're also a book of skin, a parchment upon which everything you've experienced is revealed: age lines and wrinkles, facial creases, under-eye circles brought on by fatigue, accident scars, puberty acne, the pallor of emotion. A malleable surface upon which reality imprints itself over and over, a story whose narrative can't be halted because the skin is ever affected; you can close your mouth, your eyes, plug your ears, your nose, but the skin is always available, offered, the skin can't retract, never shies away from an invitation, contact is never lost, empathy is constant, and Ninon, just imagine the torture of a total absence of stimulation, the removal of all signals from the world, imagine skin that can't feel, that's anesthetized, without nerves. Touch is the most necessary of the five senses, you can live, albeit with difficulty, blind or deaf or robbed of the ability to taste and smell, that's been seen, but you can't live without touch, that doesn't exist, it's guaranteed insanity.

Touch is the first sense to appear in a newborn, the embryo grows skin before all the other receptors, tactile contact triggers respiratory and digestive functions, then the child, the child that you once were, Ninon, learns about herself and the world through the skin, the tender and pristine surface of her body, which she experiments with constantly, touching, caressing, burning herself, grazing herself—a primitive and inaugural representation of the self, a collection of tactile perceptions that accumulate and are organized to bring forth, layer after layer, contact after contact, a consciousness, and finally an individual.

✳

You are your skin, Ninon, think about it, the skin, like all human life, is a web of contradictions, tensions, pressures, stretching and loosening, it's fragile and sensitive but also tough and elastic, watertight and porous, the cornea keeps things out and the pores open a passage; think about compromise too, and synthesis.

And so, for a few months, there are two thirty-five-minute sessions per week that don't make Ninon's symptoms disappear but do interrupt her internal monologue, guide her incessant and chaotic mental stream, even calm it a little—and talking is always a distraction, sometimes even a ruse.

Ninon enjoyed these sessions but then, given to abrupt about-faces, got bored, understanding that everything would remain at the level of hypothesis and suggestion. She didn't convert Didier Anzieu's insights into healing principles, had identified her frenzy for medical visits, her addiction to the prescription pad, hadn't decided about the extent of her responsibility or of the psychosomatic origins of her pain, in reality couldn't care less whether chance, genetics, or somatization had caused her maddening condition—undoubtedly a little bit of everything—still had the same request, make the pain stop, she once again notes the inadequacy of knowledge, reckons that she's invested herself, put her heart into it, yet she remains a miserable sack of raw skin.

If she has to choose, if no one can tell her to what extent the explanation and elucidation of a disease leads to healing, Ninon picks relief over meaning; since there's no escaping her family, which will always wield the undeniable power and authority of fact, no escaping this monolith except at the margins, by attacking from the rear, destabilizing its perpetuity, challenging tradition and disrupting its transmission, at the least, she wants to be delivered from her pain.

n Ninon Moise's family everything began in 1518 in Strasbourg, with Marie Lacaze, then her great-granddaughter Catherine Tendron was struck in her turn, the second case Esther added to the roots of the genealogical tree: Catherine, the eldest daughter of nine, religious vocation in her bones, went to Poitiers to take the veil and then suffered her own tormented iteration of the family curse, just barely escaping the stake on which people had gotten into the nasty habit of placing women at the slightest suspicion of sorcery.

Ninon was eleven, too young no doubt to hear all the nuances of this terrifying case, she burrowed beneath the covers, captivated, less by the story itself than by her mother's grave and solemn intonations.

Esther recounted that Catherine had only been shut inside the Ursuline convent for a few weeks—the pious young girl had achieved her dream—when one night at the refectory, after the last prayer of the day and lumpy leek soup, she had been seized by convulsions.

The other sisters reacted immediately, as if prepared for such an event, threw themselves on top of her, pinned her to the ground to try to calm her, but Catherine kept going, drooling even more, began to spit out gibberish, under the hold of sexual hallucinations and apparitions of ghosts with forked tails.

When the nuns loosened their grip a little, thinking her calmed, Catherine abruptly stood up and rushed at the crucifix, which she tore from the wall and, after raising her heavy dress of homespun cloth, placed inside her vagina as she laughed. No one had time to intervene; Catherine was now shamelessly masturbating with the crucifix before the paralyzed nuns, who were unable to look away. The mother superior finally shook off her stupefaction, once again threw herself at Catherine, who fell, hit the corner of a table, passed out, and was carried to her cell, where it was hoped she would remain unconscious until daybreak.

But as the night went on, though Catherine had slipped into a coma populated by scandalous images, other nuns complained of cramps in their lower stomachs, of erotic visions, and of visits by virile phantoms. At three in the morning, several of the sisters were wandering the convent corridors, clinging to one another, strolling half naked through the gardens, obscenity had taken over the Ursulines; in a few hours fifteen nuns were contaminated and madness threatened to fell the convent like syphilis in the lower clergy.

By the next day a collective exorcism had been organized, in public and in haste, at the Church of Notre Dame la Grande. The priest first turned his attention to Catherine, already renamed the "mad virgin," whom he commanded to rid herself of her demons: his voice thundered beneath the nave, he circled around her with angry eyes, blew foul-smelling air in her face, harried her—atone evil girl, witch, vile creature of the devil, or else you will perish in hell—which provoked a spectacular convulsive fit in the young nun; her body rocked back and forth with such violence that her head touched her feet, she grabbed her breasts and provocatively rubbed herself against the altar steps.

Then everything degenerated, spinning out of control, a few young girls in the curious crowd that had assembled to watch the spectacle were struck in their turn, they screamed like terrified piglets, fell into a cataplectic state, tore off their clothes, a terrible clamor rose in the church, a wave of panic swept through the parishioners, chairs were thrown into the nave, it was a melee, a scrimmage, the girls overcome by madness were taken away, people fell to their knees in prayer, crying and moaning; the church was evacuated in the confusion.

This exorcism session, far from healing and repairing, only stoked the nun's arousal and aggravated her case: in the following weeks, she developed a phantom pregnancy that she believed was caused by the insertion of the crucifix into her poor repressed body.

With little regard for Christian charity, the mother superior expelled Catherine from the Ursuline convent. She was sent to another convent in the south of France, with the hope that she wouldn't cause trouble there, but Catherine ran away a few months later and resumed a secular life, married a mussel fisherman, and in the end carried on the mad lineage by having five children, the eldest of whom was a girl.

There was that impactful, decisive, reading of Kafka's *The Metamorphosis*, then, by chance or otherwise, the day before her final session with Dr. Kilfe, another book, borrowed from the local library where Ninon liked to hang out, peruse magazines, unobtrusively observe idle men in poorly fitting parkas and MacGyvered glasses, weighed down by plastic bags, who spend their days there, in the warmth, consulting every newspaper, from the first page to the last, sometimes taking notes in a tiny spiral notebook. Lulled by the whispering, the rustling of paper, the footsteps dragging along the carpet, a calming sound bubble, Ninon dozes, kills time, sometimes leaves with a book.

This time it's a collection of essays by Fitzgerald—the title grabs her attention: *The Crack-Up*—she sits at a table, begins by skimming a few pages at random, her eyes land on a famous phrase, preserved for posterity, over-quoted, she reads it a few times to evaluate, deems it appropriate though far from welcoming, entirely adequate for what she's experiencing, a phrase calibrated for someone of her unsure age: "Of course all life is a process of breaking down."

Ninon can't be unmoved by such a maxim, she's found the original crack-up, lodged in the very principle of life, existence goes bust just like any business, over time, because since the beginning something's been incubating, advancing, growing discreetly, quietly, a tiny crack, present at birth, already splitting and eroding the earthly substance of our lives, and that something will expand, push back the shadows, eat away at us until the end. If it's determined from the start, then what's the point of fighting? If it's determined from the start, there's no particular cause for pain, no other explanation apart from life itself. What a godsend for Ninon, what consolation, this sentence is an invitation to levity and indifference, she's almost inclined to print the words on a T-shirt; in the meantime it makes her day, though not all that much because how much good can literature do a damaged body?

The next night, like so many other agitated nights, Ninon, floating within uncertain, muddied states, can't sleep and ponders pointless ideas—withdrawal from the world, a life of solitude and asceticism in a cave, an operation to remove all the nerves from her body, suicidal thoughts—strange questions—how did he feel? that first person to make an incision in someone's skin, to discover what was hiding behind it, what was hiding beneath it, that first surgeon must have been so afraid, so excited, awed, terrorized— images too, fantastical ones—Ninon removing her skin like a garment, abandoning it on the ground, an old worn-out rag—anatomical art, medical engravings of skinned bodies, cut with precision along the muscles, the skin in scraps, completely unglued, a piece of hanging laundry, or Juan Valverde de Amusco's engraving of a flayed man holding his skin in his raised hand like a shapeless costume, a ghostly disguise. Ninon had discovered this engraving from another era, which represented the skin as a shroud, during her many searches through the crevices of the internet, then she came across an excerpt from Octave Mirbeau's *Torture Garden* in which a man flayed like a rabbit, literally peeled, is dragging his skin behind him like a coat of misfortune.

During these nocturnal, immobile wanderings, transfixed by the darkness, Ninon imagines herself molting, a grass snake that grows bigger, abandons a casing that's become too tight, too cumbersome: its cold and viscous skin tears, the grass snake rubs against a stone or branch to accelerate the transition, the skin finally detaches in a single piece, is replaced by another skin, newly formed just beneath the first. Metamorphosis as salvation. Into a snake, or any other animal. Because animals have the privilege of living without skin, without that vulnerable and ridiculous envelope, protected by their scales, their fur, their wool, their hair and feathers, so much more effective, and how beautiful.

That night, half-asleep, Ninon is ready to renounce her human privileges, the superiority of her kingdom, of everything that pointlessly ranks her above an animal, and it wouldn't be a sacrifice, renouncing the complex subtlety of her brain in exchange for the toughness of leather, of a beautiful shell, armored like a safe—my brain for a rhinoceros hide, that's her evening prayer, a supplication made with hands clasped.

A year and a half has gone by, her friends have long since graduated, the seasons blur together, interactions between Ninon and her mother have gradually ceased. Esther Moise fills the fridge for her daughter, with everything she likes—tarama, chocolate mousse, mozzarella, beer—buys her newspapers and magazines, from *Elle* to *Le Monde diplomatique*, rents her DVDs, all of it placed before her bedroom door, sometimes with a handwritten note, a postcard bearing a heart or an "xoxo."

In this bedroom, shut away like Kafka's Gregor Samsa, Ninon leads a life that doesn't correspond to her age, to any age in truth, older than old, a latent life, suspended in a hazy zone where the body is just a silhouette, she's been erased from the existences of the people who once surrounded her, everything's gone dark except the skin on her arms and her brain churning like a computer, filling with images, words, sounds, a form of hyperactive depression, feverish anesthesia, a solitude full of, encumbered by even, a thousand meanderings, it's Ninon's insides that are being populated, swelling, while her outer casing remains untouched, disconnected: a bleak plain.

It's been clear for months now that medicine has failed to treat her symptom, the burning, to decipher her sick body and its encrypted grammar; Ninon is unreadable, the doctors haven't been able to translate the rumblings of her pain into a luminous and orderly string of words. So only the symptom remains, irrefutable but tautological, always pointing back at itself, without a disease to carry it, and if there's no disease, there's no recovery possible. Ninon is therefore at a standstill, dry-docked.

An endocrinologist consulted six months earlier had proclaimed: it's because people feel sick that medicine exists. Then, thanks to medicine, people know what they are sick with—a law inapplicable in Ninon's case, since feeling sick hadn't led to anything.

At this stage, the most reasonable option for Ninon would undoubtedly be to abandon the very notion of being sick, that's what Dr. Kilfe suggested, let's call it an anomaly instead, or an infirmity, something you don't recover from, without hope of regaining some supposed normality of the body, what is referred to as health, what the mustached surgeon René Leriche defined in 1935, the remote past of medicine, as the "silence of the organs"—"Health is life lived in the silence of organs." Eighty years later they haven't found anything better.

Ninon's skin isn't silent, and biological peace is an illusion; is it even possible to reach that ideal, perfectly calm and neutral state that would prepare you to endure all the breakdowns of the body, that supple and mobile state that would allow you to regain your initial form following a shock, to tolerate aggressions, to absorb irritations without lasting damage, to see them dissolved in the body's perpetual movement?

Though the world around Ninon has yet to cease reeling and crumbling, depression has gradually tempered her rebellion, dulled her anger. All that remains are two large blocks of pain and fatigue, two heaps of black peat dumped onto her bedroom carpet, two monsters who take up a lot of room but whose presence has become familiar, much less shocking, and which Ninon sometimes even observes absentmindedly. With time she's stopped ferociously resisting the pain—stiffening or rearing back only make the burning worse—letting it take possession of her body, get comfortable, making herself as transparent and light as possible, adapting, a little, to the margins, making it so the pain weighs less, she rolls up into a little ball in the storm so the lightning skirts by her, not to put up with her condition forever, that's too hard, but to cobble something together, to negotiate, perhaps the start of something else, a new phase in her quest for relief: a detachment, a form of pulling away.

For Ninon, this attempt at self-desertion, to stop caring, might save her, perhaps it's the flip side of the family millstone now heedlessly bearing down again in the wake of failure, and especially of the worry looming over her, for—this presented itself as a plausible hypothesis—can't one summon the worst by fearing it? What if dread had prompted Ninon's affliction to emerge, had desperately wished for it?

Perhaps the story of this family struck by an evil curse is one of anxiety renewed with each generation. Couldn't the worried looks of all those fathers lifting their newborns— their eldest daughters—be baleful glances that brought about sickness, looks that by way of fearing, awaiting, and tracking sickness, in fact came to desire it? introducing, accusing, and already reproaching the disaster to come. Had the weighty, provoking gaze Esther Moise directed at her child played a decisive role? And what about all those stories? Plus Ninon's own worries? Ninon who was viewed as sick by her mother before she ever was, viewed as the bearer of tragedy before it could even unfurl.

This is the conclusion, which granted is not very rational for a girl who claims to be so, reached by Ninon, the kind a person could in good faith allow themselves to reach after months of pain, hundreds of hours shut up in a bedroom or lying on a bed in uncomfortable positions. Her mother's anxious—but also excited, agitated, impatient—gaze might be the evil eye that eventually, grandly, summoned Ninon's affliction. It's a hypothesis, and one that could mark the ultimate vanquishing of reason, in any case it's a new way of considering the situation, of starting things up again, the point not being to heal—the term has become unsuitable—but to regain some semblance of self.

Let's imagine then that it will no longer be a question of healing but of undoing the curse. Let's accept, at the same time, that sticking with science demands a minimum of physical fitness, energy, hope. Let's acknowledge that Ninon is far too tired, far too weary to not let herself drift toward more uncertain zones.

t's a small flyer, printed in blurry green ink, which Ninon picked up at the exit of the Barbès metro station months ago now. She held onto the unassuming prospectus, tacked it above her desk, looks at it often, deciphering the compressed, barely legible words:

Specialist in affairs of the heart. Unfailing ability to bring loved ones back. Your husband or wife leave you? They will come running after you like a dog behind its master thanks to my supernatural gifts. Resolve your family issues and money and relationship problems. Even disappointed by another psychic. Protection against all dangers. Sexual issues. Unknown disease. Driver's license. Exams, loneliness, fertility, luck, success in all your projects and endeavors. Unenchantments. Rapidity and efficiency are the foundations of my work. Pure and sincere medium. Lifetime guarantees. Discretion assured.

Above the list of the marabout's services and fields of expertise, a tiny, dark photo—a black face deep in concentration, topped with a white kufi—offers a visualization of Monsieur Bana. The image is accompanied by a caption: *great seer medium is among you! satisfaction in 48h top. Available every day by appointment.* Ninon, for fun, for a laugh, and you never know, had called the number several times though without success, systematically reaching a voice mail box that didn't take messages and happily played conga music instead.

Now she mechanically rereads the flyer and her eyes linger on "unknown disease" then "unenchantment," she wonders which of these two misfortunes is the right one, is hers, the pretext for contacting Monsieur Bana. If she finally managed to get him on the phone, what would she say was the reason for her call? Hello, I'm calling about an unknown disease? or hello Monsieur Bana, it's for an unenchantment. Ninon tells herself that after all perhaps Monsieur Bana is a doctor who missed his calling, who failed his college entrance exam, or that all the doctors she's consulted are unknowingly also Banas—their hermetic speech, orders in the form of riddles, and prescriptions written in illegible handwriting all create a world as murky and secret as Monsieur Bana's magic spells. On both sides the patient is asked to enthusiastically submit to some authority, to have faith in order to be healed. Didn't medicine start with magic? Doesn't it come from that very obscurity? Ninon, at this stage, categorically decides that there's a thin line between medicine and the occult, easily crossed when all the gods of the religion of science are dead, when nothing remains except experimentation and its infinite possibilities.

Ninon is ready. Prepared to change tack. Now that she's passed through the cogs of a machine and the hands of a psychiatrist. Ripe for magical thinking, a contemporary and voluntaristic version of the faith of her ancestors, the Lacazes, the Millots, the Tendrons, the Quignes, the Lamousses, the Flanchets, all devoted believers from whom Ninon will take the baton, though instead of a fool, she'll play the fighter, an ironic pout on her lips.

The year she turned fourteen, Ninon and her mother spent a weekend in Marseilles. They rented a room in the Vieux-Port, ate ice cream in the old quarter, went swimming in the Calanques, visited the Vieille Charité Museum, then climbed to the top of the city, all the way to the Notre Dame de la Garde Basilica, where La Bonne Mère watches over sailors, the soccer players of the Olympique de Marseille, and all the city's residents. They admired the impressive collection of ex-votos offered to the Virgin to thank her for an act of mercy. The walls were covered with those small marble plaques, mineral postcards engraved with wishes for protection, help, success, or healing. They read dozens of them out loud, condensed tales of adventure, pseudo-novellas, vehicles for dreaming, and Ninon and her mother together imagined the lives contained in these sparse, chiseled words:

December 4, 1901 in the Indian Ocean lost at sea and assailed by a terrible cyclone. Grateful to Notre Dame de la Garde for saving us.
Commander A.F. Mattéi

Marie gives thanks to the Bonne Mère because her son Marin did not poison himself when he swallowed some pills. January 21, 1985.

Thank you Bonne Mère for sending a cure to my sheep for they were dying of a terrible disease with no remedy to be found and now they are doing well (Paul Nuevo, 1947).

José, fisherman, expresses his gratitude to the Bonne Mère for granting him health after the pain in his hands and for giving him strength to continue working on the high seas. Blessed be the fishing for which she saved me.
March 1950.

They then went out onto the cathedral square to admire the view and Esther Moise took a package in bubble wrap out of her purse, handing it to her daughter with a satisfied smile—a present!—Ninon accepted it reluctantly, tore off the wrapping, discovered a plaque the size of a half sheet of A4 paper, a white marble rectangle on which was engraved in gold capital letters: BONNE MÈRE, PROTECT NINON, THANK YOU.

Now we have to find a place to put it, Esther burst out laughing, Ninon was embarrassed then stiffened, paralyzed by the feeling that she was looking at her own gravestone, reproduced in miniature, engraved with an absurd epitaph. Seeing her daughter's annoyance, Esther thought better, presented the ex-voto as a quirky gift, a Dadaist gesture—Ninon didn't understand the word *Dadaist* but her mother's flippancy and nonchalance struck her as partially feigned, she already knew Esther was a little off and now suspected her of secretly believing in miracles.

✳

Remembering this story five years later, Ninon tells herself that in the end making that direct plea to the Virgin couldn't have hurt, wonders if the wish could never be granted because she had refused to place the ex-voto in view of all the Basilica's visitors, can't help but think that if the plaque had been mounted for eternity in the heights of Marseilles she wouldn't be in this position today, and then swats away the thought like a fly.

The ex-voto ended up in a dresser drawer as soon as they returned home, amid a jumble of knickknacks and half-empty cigarette packs. Ninon looks everywhere in the apartment for it, doesn't find it, her mother no doubt got rid of it eventually, the joke stopped being funny; the curse had struck.

Ninon sits in front of her computer, looks for something, someone toward which she can redirect her lost, betrayed trust, is now avidly searching the internet for the contact details of a sorcerer, an exorcist, then a shaman, types *trance*, types *shaman therapist paris* and, indeed, no need to travel to the steppes of Mongolia or the Amazonian rainforest, there are Parisian shamans ready to see her in two-bedroom apartments near the Place d'Italie.

She opens the door in socks, a detail that doesn't escape Ninon or work in the shaman's favor; she goes by Asha. The rest of her outfit is sober, no sorceress garb, talismans around her neck, puffy non-Western clothing. Sixtyish, olive skin, black turtleneck tight against her body, which is tall and slender, and a digital watch on her wrist.

She asks Ninon to take her shoes off, invites her in with an enticing voice, a voice typical of a therapist—Ninon can now spot these particular inflections, these intonations specific to those who heal, whose function is to listen and offer relief, these smooth and authoritative accents, calming and resolute; she knows them by heart.

In the main room dedicated to the shamanic treatment, there is a striking contrast between the modern, functional layout (roller blinds, sprung floor, sliding picture windows, halogen lights in the drop ceiling) and an impressive cabinet of curiosities that occupies the entire width of the back wall: behind the glass, a collection of anthropomorphic figurines, African dolls, amulets preserved in vials of red oil, humanoid faces sculpted from pieces of wood, a magical Kanak stone shaped like a brain or maybe a cloud—a concretion of magnesia that comes from Houaïlou in New Caledonia, explains the shaman—and offerings arranged on a tray of sculpted ivory, a kind of miniature altar: dried beef blood in a tiny bowl, a small glass of white alcohol, a few coffee beans, a cone of rolling tobacco.

Ninon is encouraged to admire each of these treasures at length, this is part of the preparation, but also they have to wait for nightfall because nightfall is when the spirits are more powerful.

Fifteen minutes later, after a spiced black tea and answering Ninon's invariably pressing questions—about her shamanic syncretism, which invokes Denetsak, the forest spirit of the Trumai Indians of Brazil, as often as it does the wandering souls of the Siberian steppe—the shaman of the thirteenth arrondissement has her patient lie down on a floor mat in the middle of the room, asks her to close her eyes, to let herself go, to let herself be guided. Ninon tries to sink into the thin rubber mat, to release the tension in her body, to push her eyeballs into the back of their sockets like Asha tells her, to melt her temples into her cranium and slide the skin from the front of her ears to the back, to breathe from her lower body, to feel her intestines beating with the in-breath and the out-breath, and to think of nothing.

The shaman kneels and whispers: let the spirits come, let them multiply; really feel their presence; liberate your soul from the weight of your inhabited body; the spirits will manifest themselves through a series of sensations or perceptions hosted by your body; the spirits' presence will envelop you like a second skin, soothing yours.

The shamanic healing session will last thirty minutes, the room is now dark with shadows, dimly lit by a single candle, a stick of sage is burning to purify the space and the patient. The shaman sits cross-legged a few feet away from Ninon, wedges her Siberian drum between her thighs, stops moving for an instant, ceremoniously, then begins to vigorously play, her hand descends, strikes the stretched skin in rhythm, each beat accompanied by a loud exclamation that, upon reaching Ninon's eardrums, forms the strange word *dungur*: dungur! dungur! dungur! Ninon started the first time, inhales the exquisite smell of sage, looks out for incoming signs.

The enchanting and sustained drum rhythm is meant to induce the trance, the sound is meant to bring forth the spirits, presences only accessible through the instrument's frequencies, which manifest in the form of magnetic inductions.

The shaman is still drumming—dungur! dungur!—the plant burns up, the darkness thickens, Ninon goes numb, then feels a cold wind go through her, feels it or dreams it, her heartbeat accelerates gradually along with her pulse, each drum sound prompting a slight muscular contraction somewhere in her body, tiny short circuits—stomach, arms, thighs, calves—but Ninon remains impassive, observes these odd electrical sensations from inside herself, as somber as a coal mine.

The first session is over, Ninon couldn't say how long it lasted, an ungraspable, rubbery duration; the shaman sets down her bewitching drum, covers it with a cloth, kneels beside Ninon, whose eyes are still shut, her breathing now slow and deep in her belly, she barely quivers when she senses the woman's proximity, her hands floating and dancing several inches above her patient's body, from top to bottom.

The shaman begins to breathe noisily with her mouth, head back, lapping the air, then spits into a small earthen bowl placed at Ninon's feet—she hears her expectorate but remains focused, trying to respect the exercise to the end, to follow the rules, adhere; Ninon is a serious girl—I'm breathing in the black stains hanging over the room, these stains are evil, they are the evil inside you, I'm extracting it, ingesting it, expulsing it, I'm neutralizing it by mixing it with my saliva and my breath.

Don't open your eyes no matter what, do not move, I'm going to lie down next to you and proceed to soul retrieval— the therapist's voice is growing distant, underwater— we'll start by finding your animal-totem.

Ninon feels Asha's fragrant body brush against her, a light scent of amber, the armadillo or porcupine are your totems; Ninon didn't understand, only grasped the syllables, floating, solitary sounds, ar, ma, dil, o, por, ki, pine, that don't form any words, anything intelligible. The shaman had said it before the start of the trance: all reality has two sides, two dimensions, tangible and intangible, and the sound of the Siberian drum will guide us to the intangible side. Then a vague physical sensation rises in Ninon, the kind you feel in a half sleep, when the flesh is slowed down, when the outside world fades away, bodily senses switching off and others—internal, incorporeal, previously unknown—awakening. Now she has the troubling and uncertain feeling that her aliveness stems from a point buried deep within her body, somewhere between the liver and the spinal column, that her visceral core, what Philippe Tissié called the *moi splanchnique*, is swelling, taking up room, an interior life is manifesting, this is the goal sought by the shaman: we're here.

In a shamanic trance, the patient is led by stages toward a kind of nocturnal state, so that the site where information is received is no longer found on the surface of the body— pupils, nostrils, eardrums, skin—but inside; surveillance of the world is disabled and the patient, as if asleep, can still hear but poorly (scrambled sounds), can see but vaguely (halos of light), can feel but in a blurred way, while the viscera become the neuralgic center, the receptor of emotions and sensations—and it's precisely this intermediary state that Ninon, it would seem, has just reached.

The shaman struck seven drumbeats four times, signaling the end of the session, the emergence from the trance. Ninon opens her eyes, her body stiff, filaments luminous, head buzzing, and instantaneously: the burning contact of the mat against her arms, undulating red sparks dancing on her skin, the familiarity with the pain.

A few minutes later she's composed herself, rolls gently to one side, stands up, puts on her shoes, hands over seventy euros in cash—money always procured in abundance by her mother—robotically says thank you, feels pretty good, light and a little tipsy, despite the ever present, arrogant, unoustable symptom.

You'll have to wait a few days to see if your skin proves to be less sensitive, I extracted a good number of harmful elements from your body; powerful animal spirits visited you during the treatment, take some time to think about the armadillo and the porcupine again, think about their skin.

After the chorus of doctors, the time of the shamans has come. Ninon begins a new round of treatments, somewhat reenergized by these novel experiences, always embarked upon with the same tenacity and soon the same skepticism—one not excluding the other—but she persists as usual, all the more so as she finds some respite, diversion, a few ecstatic moments of relief, interludes. Every session, depending on methods that vary little, entails lying down, letting herself go, breathing in heady smells, emptying herself, listening in a daze to a repetitive series of sounds and words, feeling the rhythm, heartbeats and drumbeats, enduring various manipulations of her joints, some light twisting of her neck, hands placed on her stomach, near the liver or gallbladder.

The benefit of these shamanic sessions is that they exhaust Ninon, a new kind of exhaustion; she emerges unsteady each time, worn out, at best battered by a fatigue whose origin, finally, is no longer her monstrous pain but the more or less mysterious actions of a sorcerer; diversifying the source of her exhaustion is already a help to Ninon, the start of repair, of taking things in hand.

After visiting various apartment-based Parisian shamans, more or less fantastical, high-strung or very solemn, adherents of yogic, Indian, Nenet, or Mongolian teachings, and after experiencing states of rest and of agitation of varying intensity, Ninon, climbing an exponential and addictive slope, aspires to even more radical and unsettling experiences, far from the reassuring and confined spaces of indoor shamans—and when it comes to those kinds of extremes, it's the internet once again that offers unlimited access; all she has to do is plunge into an ordered maze of sites and hyperlinks, follow the trail, the offshoots and footnotes, and each click is another step into the thick fog of knowledges and practices. To Ninon, who's withdrawn from the physical world, the internet is the most living she can do.

This is how she eventually digs up a healer whose homepage, without flourishes or photos, written in a style she judges impeccable, convinces her immediately. Shamanism is described in terms of the therapeutic use of magic, of our bodies and the way they are all connected, of the disturbances of reality that echo inside us, of the somatic halos then produced, of disease as a disruptive power that breaks the harmony with nature, and expresses the spirits' ire and disapproval, and of healing that puts the broken body back together, and which isn't the annihilation of pain but a negotiation to reestablish the broken pact, the lost understanding, thanks to a dialogue with the spirits that can only be led by the healer, shaman, voodoo priest, neither men nor gods but mediators, intercessors between two worlds, the visible and the hidden, standing at the threshold, vibrating to terrestrial forces and celestial manifestations.

The healer claims to come from a forest in the Amazon and officiates in one west of Paris: Rambouillet Forest. You register online, pay in advance, one hundred and fifty euros, vegetarian picnic included, you're summoned a few days later to the metro stop Porte d'Auteuil at ten p.m., and advised to dress in warm, comfortable clothes. The website provides scant information about how the treatment will proceed—an individual section and a group section, ingestion of a beverage, a disclaimer to sign, return early in the morning.

It's May, a nice night, a minibus with glazed windows is waiting for the dozen participants to drive them to the forest. Ninon arrived a little early, gave her name to the driver, who looks peaky, like a plucked heron, he checked her off the list, then she observes the other supplicants out of the corner of her eye, has no desire to talk, to exchange, has lost the ability to be with others; they range between forty and sixty years old, some appear to know one another, dressed in fleece jackets, ankle boots, wind pants—as if for a hike—they're excited and demonstrative. Ninon finds them ridiculous, considers herself just as ludicrous among them, imagines they're librarians, teachers, or artisans, she hunkers down in the back of the bus, headphones in her ears, sporting that stubborn look that never leaves her.

At this time of night the drive is smooth all the way to Rambouillet Forest, then the bus driver guides them along a narrow trail, single file and in silence broken only by the hooting of an owl, the cracking of twigs, they learn that the shaman is waiting at the end of that trail, they are impatient and apprehensive, they find a massive teepee made of animal skins erected beneath the moon.

The healing session is taking place in the forest because spirits don't like the city, don't like light and electricity, because in the city spirits collide with an invisible wall: the immaterial world in which we bathe unawares and vulnerable, the world of electromagnetic waves, viruses, carbon dioxide, harmful air that saturates everything and stops the spirits from showing themselves. Here, in the forest, the spirits have the best possible conditions, the forest is the most favorable setting for them to manifest—this invisible something that we're seeking, that you're seeking tonight, is characterized by the fact that it reveals itself, only to certain people and under certain conditions, but it does reveal itself, penetrating the visible world; it can be perceived.

The shaman spoke, and everyone listened with exaggerated respect. He's seated cross-legged in the center of the teepee, prematurely wrinkled, long hair swept up in a bun on the top of his head, full beard; he's wearing combat fatigues, leather sandals, and a cotton tunic. He indicates that the participants should sit in a circle, on large pillows filled with massage beads.

Ninon's alert gaze takes in everything: a brazier, whose smoke escapes through a small zinc chimney, is glowing in one corner, a samovar is set on a camping table, storm lamps provide weak lighting, dozens of objects clutter the teepee (kitchen utensils, sculpted faces with ferocious eyes, voodoo totems), a long stick adorned with charms (feathers, nails, cords, eagle claws, and a duck beak) is planted in the ground and at the foot of the stick, a calabash filled with oil. Attached to the teepee's central pillar are ram horns that ward off danger, hedgehog spikes that protect from injury, and a dried frog skin that brings peace and fertility.

The shaman is now brandishing a voodoo statue approximately three feet high, calls for silence among the group, which is attentive and a little lost, and begins with a suave and decided voice—that therapist voice that Ninon again identifies at the first note: I want you to admire this shea wood statuette covered with small padlocks, note in particular these linked ones placed around the ears, chest, and pelvis. Be aware that the statuette was coated in sacrificial blood to provoke various ailments in an adversary—mutism, suffocation, stomach pain, sterility. Pay equal attention to the mirror shards, pearls, teeth, and in particular the ropes and chains binding the body like shackles. The ropes around the lower belly destroy sexual power, the ones around the chest impede breathing, the leg ones paralyze, the neck ones cause aphasia, and finally this small animal jaw tied to the abdomen is intended to silence an inconvenient witness. If you remove the locks, if you undo all the ropes, then your enemy can speak again and his suffering will end.

The group sinks a little deeper into the silence and the large bead-filled cushions, outside barely a rustle of night air; faces are drawn, from fatigue and excitement, and reddened by the enveloping heat of the brazier, it smells like musk and heather, Ninon shivers, vaguely anxious, isn't thinking in that moment of the pain on her skin, of her jean shirt touching her arms, but is wondering what's in the paper bag that the bus driver handed to her earlier as he was calling roll: chips and a banana or some psychotropic plant ground to powder to accelerate the trance?

Here's how it's going to go: you will spend the night in this teepee, keeping warm; you're welcome to lie down, relax, sleep if you feel like it, serve yourself some hibiscus juice from the samovar, talk quietly if you're craving interaction. I'll come get you one by one, in alphabetical order, for the healing session that will take place outside, then I'll bring you back to the teepee. And the bus will drop you off at Porte d'Auteuil tomorrow morning around seven a.m.

As she waits for her turn, Ninon lies down on a synthetic bearskin near the brazier, soon dozes off, lulled by whispers. It's four a.m. when the shaman calls her name— Ninon Moise, please—she gets up at once, rubs her eyes, responds with a nod, they leave in silence. Outside the air is cool, sharp and fragrant, reinvigorating, Ninon follows the shaman who disappears into the forest without turning around, head down, with a hunter's agile gait.

They say you have to believe in magic for it to work, but isn't it by carrying out religious rituals that you end up finding your faith? Repetition becomes habit, becomes second nature then first nature, the body leads the mind, swept up in the motion—by doing, you believe in what you're doing—and so Ninon acts, is content with action, begins in this moment to mirror the healer, makes a series of gestures, moves her body and receives, in proportion to these movements, sensory information, emotions that are events, she is an assemblage of pistons and conveyer belts, a machine subject to forces, intensities, and fluids; and having faith or not won't change anything of this mechanistic operation.

Ninon doesn't ask herself whether the invisible world evoked by the shaman truly exists, whether spirits are made up; they are a chance at a new experience and that's all that matters. If the invisible world can be perceived, she'll find out soon enough, her body will feel it beneath the trees of Rambouillet Forest. She's cold, the night is crackling, the ground is loose under their feet, the shaman's firm voice echoes: greetings to he or she who comes to unravel the mystery of all that is intertwined, each time a knot is undone a god is released. A crow lets out a terrible caw, Ninon's eyes get used to the darkness, the black turns gray and blue, she's never seen that before, therefore the magic has begun to work.

They reach a clearing, beneath a weak crescent moon, face one another, Ninon follows the healer's silent directions, a few motions and looks, they get on their knees one yard apart from one another. The shaman finally speaks, asks

Ninon to share, what brings you here? And Ninon shares, speaks simply, leaves nothing out, her family, the doctors, the failed treatments, the solitude, in detail, a long monologue, encouraged by the shaman's approving murmurs.

When she stops talking, he grabs her hands: you offended a spirit and I'm going to try and repair that affront, to appease the malevolent spirit, to restore harmony, the evil isn't in you but around you, the evil is in the broken link.

Despite her unfailing willingness, in this moment Ninon disconnects, smothers a laugh deep in her throat—some guy disguised as a sorcerer is earnestly looking her straight in the eyes, an idiotic trap she got herself into, the cold, the night, the hostile forest, make-believe.

She immediately forces herself to come back, to resume her role, gazes at the beautiful starry sky, takes a deep breath, focuses, on the reason she's here, her allodynia that defies all explanation—her rejection of the family curse, a failure of the medical logic that assigns a cause to every effect—her pointless suffering about which she tries, a real trooper, not to think too much about to avoid going crazy.

And Ninon composes herself, melts back into the darkness, the forest, the song of nocturnal birds, the voice of this man—shaman, sorcerer, magician, or healer, it doesn't matter—who is now suggesting she resituate her life within an intricate web of meaning, not the narrow, monolithic one of genealogy or symptomology, but the limitless web of earth and sky, expanded to include plants, animals, spirits, ghosts, and the dead. Whereas the doctors methodically isolated her, diagnosed her as a unique, unsolvable case, tonight the shaman is offering to reconnect her to the rest of the world, to finally return her to the heart of the surrounding chaos.

They're still kneeling across from one another, Ninon, numb, begins to squirm, the shaman releases her hands but maintains eye contact: Ninon, remember that intuition is the language through which the spirits send us messages, we have to listen, if you don't follow your intuition you'll arouse their anger, and they will cause you endless suffering to clearly express that anger, they will scream so that this time you hear them, so that you finally pay attention. The spirits are screaming in your skin. It's your intuition that's failing and together we're going to revive it.

After a moment, necessary no doubt for the words to penetrate Ninon's spongy matter, the shaman asks her to push up her shirtsleeves and show her skin. Your pain is invisible—no trace on the surface of your arms—that's why only the invisible world can fight it. The solution is invisible too, intangible and undetectable.

The shaman claps his hands, a surprised blackbird flies away, he finally motions to Ninon to stand up, then stretches out yawning: the treatment will occur in two stages, follow me.

They take another narrow path, two hundred yards long, hemmed in by a forest that's growing darker, reach a second clearing, with the circumference of a small circus ring and in the middle of which a hole has been dug, like a shallow grave—twenty inches deep, six feet long, barely three feet wide. Starting now you need to be silent, let go, follow my instructions, and everything will be fine.

Ninon is asked to lie down in this hole, the bottom of which has been carpeted with moss and ferns. She does this without apprehension, now entirely focused, she feels the moisture through her clothes, painful pressure on the backs of her arms, which she crosses over her chest, she closes her eyes, the shaman then covers her body with a thin layer of dirt, Ninon doesn't protest, he takes a kind of percussion rattle out of his pants pocket, an *asson* apparently, made from a gourd wrapped in strings of bones, pearls, and shells.

Ninon breathes in the fragrant forest air, sinks into her humus bed as the shaman plays the asson and dances around the hole, pounding the ground with heavy steps, announces that he's going to create a wave of vibrations—the nature surrounding us vibrates due to the continuous movement of electrons, I'm going to capture those vibrations, redirect them toward you, so that you vibrate again, so that contact with others, with their skin, makes you vibrate—he strikes the ground even harder, shakes the asson in rhythm, accelerating the movements of his syncopated dance, circles Ninon, who is fearless, attentive, hopeful, looking out for the slightest manifestation of her body that for now isn't expressing anything other than the usual burning in her arms, and so the shaman plays, runs, and dances faster and faster, whipping the air, a vibration finally rises, an ondulatory vortex born from the colliding of bones as the shaman leaps in the air and then returns to the ground, space begins to tremble discreetly, the night whirling, at least that's how it seems to Ninon, the shaman spins around and around, Ninon cries out like a strangled nestling, feels herself vibrating, a soft wave at first, weak voltage that makes her skin crackle, then more intense tremors, spasms in her belly and limbs, Ninon clenches her fists, holds her breath for fear she'll lose the sensation, hangs on to it, offers herself to the electricity, the shaman vocalizes, a groan from deep in his chest, inarticulate guttural sounds that accompany the asson beats, and Ninon lets out an involuntary grunt, she doesn't recognize her voice, barely realizes that this noise has come out of her body, snorts, a final shudder then she slides into a dark and distant pocket above the trees, a cocoon, curls up then unfolds, enchanted by the strange but comforting sensation of an animal metamorphosis, her legs like a wolf's, thin and muscular, her nose widening and lengthening like a snout, fur covering her body, forming a second skin, warm and protective, a feeling of bursting and reforming, of dispossession and rebirth in another body, a giddiness that grows, then the tears, the shaman was expecting them, a flood accompanied by hiccups, loud snotty sniffles, Ninon lets the pain and fatigue float away.

The shaman is lying beside the hole, just above his patient. Ninon can hear him breathing noisily, panting, this goes on for a while, they're both coming out of it, their heartbeats finally blending into the nocturnal peace of the forest.

Are you going to be okay, Ninon? Can we proceed to the second stage of the treatment?

Ninon struggles to sit up, wipes away her tears, I'm fine, she rises, dazed, gets herself out of the hole, on her hands and knees at first, it seems to her that the night is beginning to wane—shades of gray and purple emerging—that dawn is close, she takes a few steps, tottering on her restored human legs, but she's no longer cold.

The shaman grabs her wrist, come on it's not far, they walk, shakily, to a tiny hut made of branches and ferns that you have to enter hunched over like it's an igloo. Inside there's only room if you're seated, three or four people at most, Ninon sits cross-legged, tries to pull herself together, the shaman takes a flashlight out of his back pocket and points it at a chest hidden beneath a few branches, inside are two fleece blankets, a bottle full of copper-colored liquid, and two shot glasses.

Holding the flashlight between his teeth, he carefully opens the bottle and fills the two glasses, we're going to drink ayahuasca together, it's a therapeutic brew made from bark and vine stems, you'll see it's a little bitter at first but you get used to it quickly. Ninon, nervous this time, asks where the bottle came from and what does it do. You don't have to be afraid, we're going to drink it together, it comes from the Amazon, it's meant to purge you and awaken your failing intuition, trust me it's a reputed beverage, used by shamans around the world for centuries.

Ninon, still weak and confused, warily takes the glass, the shaman takes a first sip, so she gulps hers down, the harsh juice of the Amazonian jungle makes her violently gag, but she still has to take two more doses to ensure it will work.

They drank it all, the liquid leaves a disagreeable and lingering taste in Ninon's mouth, they crawl out of the hut, they wrap themselves in the blankets, it will take thirty minutes for the ayahuasca to kick in, they wait huddled up several feet apart, staring into space.

Ninon's afraid, asks herself what she's doing here, what got into her, waits for the damn drink to take effect, wishes she could exchange a few words with the shaman who's closed his eyes and isn't moving, rolled into a ball. She watches the minutes pass, gently rocking back and forth, when suddenly it hits, swells, swarms even, white spots before her eyes digging holes in the darkness, multicolored moving visions, golden filaments, the trance beginning again, this time triggering hypertrophy of the senses, her vision sharpened and hearing amplified, Ninon hears ants crawling on the bark, the sound of a falling leaf, the crackling of moon beams, she's cold again—the creepy sensation of being covered by snakes with viscous, icy skin—then too hot, is overcome by terror then courage, switches from one state to the next in a fragment of a second, her body feels like it has evaporated, all her organs dissolved in the night, Ninon is just a brain floating between the tree branches observing the world, honed, lying in wait for her prey, ready to release her arrow, a gelatinous, weightless mass, light, mobile, hyper-lucid.

She feels herself melt, disappear, then fly; ecstasy. But three minutes later it's the fall, her body abruptly reforms, returns to its terrestrial place, dense and heavy, a sack of sand, it inflates, stretches to the edges of the forest, explodes beyond its limits, rips its envelope, exceeding the narrow expanse of flesh and blood demarcated by the skin, and finally expands to the dimensions of the mind—how can our tightly restricted bodies house such vast minds?

This abyss of a question doesn't have time to enter Ninon's awareness because she begins to vomit; the ayahuasca is having its purge effect—the details of which the shaman deliberately withheld—the vomiting signals the end of the trance, the expulsion of evil, the return to normalcy. A few yards away the shaman is vomiting as well, convulsing, Ninon panics, he's chalky pale, his face twisted by pain; he reassures her with a hand motion, don't worry, turns away.

Ninon gave up on any human exchanges long ago, but in this moment, she's no longer alone in the world, and is full of gratitude for the shaman, for his commitment, for their communal, shared suffering, which overwhelms her, she thinks of all those doctors who impressed her so, distant and disembodied authority figures, of their knowledge that she now finds very cold, and she looks at this man holding his stomach, this concrete, powerful man who invested his body alongside hers, danced to exhaustion, drank ayahuasca with her, who's still spitting up acidic bile in the hope that she'll be healed, she mumbles a few emotional thank-yous, smiles shyly at him, they're feeling better now, lying in the fetal position beneath their blankets, they take a few more minutes, we're done, the treatment is over, Ninon.

*

They return along the same path, Ninon, still nauseous, again trails the shaman whose silhouette grows more distinct as the sun rises, describes to him as best she can the sensations she experienced during the trance, the tremors, the dissociation, the animal, the hallucinations, as he walks with increasing steadiness. At the teepee entrance, the shaman warmly shakes Ninon's hand, congratulates her, for her bravery, her resistance to the cruelty of her pain, whispers a few words in her ear, and disappears. There's still a little time to warm up, eat and drink, rest before taking the bus back to Paris, everyone's asleep inside the teepee, bodies heavy, sleep agitated, Ninon serves herself a hibiscus infusion from the samovar, bolts down her picnic lunch, nuts and a cucumber-Swiss sandwich, can't believe what she just lived through, even if it's already becoming fuzzy in her mind, taking on the uncertain texture of a dream, and though only the foul taste of ayahuasca attests that something unusual did indeed happen.

The small group so excited upon leaving Paris is unnerved and grim-faced when they're dropped off at Porte d'Auteuil, it's eight a.m., everyone disperses without a word or look, all in a rush to return to their rooms, their beds, to find themselves alone so they can get a handle on the strange night, reflect on it calmly, to assure themselves they haven't gone completely mad, that they are still on this side of life.

Ninon dozes in a fold-down metro seat, indifferent to the mass of travelers pressing in around her, she feels the burning touch of her still damp shirt against her skin, the pain growling, she's too exhausted to react, and isn't surprised, wasn't really expecting to be healed, for the moment she's satisfied with, and settles for, the experience—waves of sensations and mystery, modified states of consciousness, broadened physical capabilities, the introduction of other types of pain, and once again the relief at hurting somewhere else, a restorative diverting of attention, a circuit rerouted to other zones of the self.

Soothed by the strident swaying of the metro car, galvanized by her sleepless, hallucinatory night, Ninon feels full of strength and audacity, bathed in the prestige of the ordeal, and in this moment, not far from happy.

Ninon's not healed, of course, but is healing still the objective?

The shaman had warned them about intelligence, about the arrogance and complacency of that self-sustaining machine, and recommended reinforcing the intuitive brain and slowing the speculative brain. Ninon doesn't quite see how to invert the two, or really what the shaman meant, but what she's been feeling from the beginning, from the very first morning, is in fact an intensification of her cerebral faculties, high on hits of reality triggered by the pain.

She hasn't slept in over twenty-four hours, just spent a grueling night in the forest, finally lies down on her bedroom carpet, eyes closed, focused on her breath, recalls a belly breathing exercise, breathe in and the stomach swells, breathe out and it retracts, the belly button sinks, stretches toward the ground, breathe in breathe out in search of the perfect loop, of a continuous motion, without interruption, slow and steady, until your breathing becomes imperceptible, a miniscule action of the body, the mind turned off, skin relaxed, reduced to the act of respiration, in order to diminish yourself, make your existence as discreet as possible, and perhaps clear a path to intuition.

One looming presence marked Ninon's childhood, a particularly impressive, and disruptive, figure of the family curse—Louise Tempe, mother of Esther Moïse—perhaps the most beautiful and most admirable figure to emerge from this profusion of wild tales, from this disarray over which madness reigned, haunting every woman from the moment she gave birth to her first daughter.

For Ninon, this singular and mysterious grandmother served as oracle, magician, and sovereign of an invisible and parallel world—and her story is incredible.

Louise Tempe was struck in a particularly cruel way, by permanent vision and hearing loss. She went blind and deaf abruptly, a few weeks after her fifteenth birthday, for no known medical reason. The world retreated, she had to learn to live deprived of two of her five senses, to live in silence and darkness, to continue speaking though unable to hear, to continue interpreting reality though unable to see.

Ninon loved this heroic and rigid grandmother, who always comported herself correctly, regally, who spoke in a slow, fragmented voice, unable to access her own words except in the form of slight vibrations, which would prompt her extinguished eyes, round and heavy as taws, to spin.

Louise used to say that deaf people don't live in absolute silence, that a constant noise fills their brains, which takes on varying hues and frequencies depending on the time of day and one's mood, which ranges from a very slight hissing to, at worst, a screeching that builds to a whistle; she used to say that sometimes the noise is so deafening that you think you're going mad, that you shake your head every which way, that you dunk it in water to make it stop.

She also told Ninon that blind people never find themselves in total darkness, that distinctive tones enter their fields of vision, plumes of color, bright dots, somewhat faded stains that, though you wish you could stare at them at length, disappear immediately, that a multitude of minor events are occurring in a blind person's pupils, in a deaf person's eardrums, at every single moment. She did her best to explain blindness to a child, to convey that irreducible experience, and it was as if she were reciting a poem, she compared it to a deep and opaque river that flows slowly for thousands of miles, silent, calm, and ends in a large black lake, she also spoke of waves and jets of water that some-times trouble the surface of the lake—the violent panic attacks of the blind, she called them.

Louise Tempe frequented others who were trapped inside their bodies, referred to them as her fellow sufferers, she would grab their hands, giving a long squeeze before bringing them to her head so they could decode the shape of her face, discover the form of her skull, appraise the texture of her hair, then she'd do the same, palpating in her turn, she would take these companions in her arms and by the hand, always maintaining contact, for when the eyes no longer see, when the ears no longer hear, a hand is all that allows you not to lose the world, her hand always placed on someone else's—letting go meant being projected hundreds of miles away, meant a bottomless well of solitude, meant an abrupt detour out of the land of the living.

Her veined, manicured hands, which Ninon used to examine like they were treasures, had become the most essential of organs, all speech passing through the skin, and to communicate Louise Tempe had learned a complex digital alphabet, written on the palm. When her capacities were diminished, far from feeling discouraged, Louise set out to memorize this tactile form of com-munication, the Lorm alphabet, as quickly as possible: a series of lines and dots on the inside of the hand represent letters; the palm and fingers are covered with invisible keys, to which are applied light pressure—you tap, graze, caress, pat to form words, meanings.

Louise first taught this language to her husband, René Moise, who was perfectly able-bodied but died prematurely at fifty-five in a car accident, then to her daughter, Esther, and finally—a few rudiments—to her granddaughter, Ninon. Now remember that the A is a tap on the tip of the thumb, that you make the G with a short stroke in the middle of the ring finger, the P with a long upward stroke on the outside of the index finger, the S by tracing a circle in the palm, that K is a tap with four fingertips on the palm, the Z a diagonal line from the base of the thumb to the base of the little finger—an alphabet that demands great concentration to instantaneously identify the placement of each letter, string them together, and compose sentences. While her grandmother could write seventy-five syllables per minute, Ninon could barely form thirty, but that was enough to communicate a few pieces of information and a few sentiments, reduced to the essential.

The deaf Louise also liked to take her granddaughter to concerts; she would detect the vibrations of the wind and string instruments, then grab her granddaughter's arm and beat time. Sometimes Louise would ask Ninon to ring a bell next to her ear, or place a radio, volume up all the way, on her stomach, so she could feel the sound waves pulsating in her intestines.

Louise constantly wanted to touch and taste and feel, she was inordinately fond of whiskey, the smell of incense, the heat and the cold, dryness and humidity, sea bathing and wind, she liked botanical gardens, especially brushing against the cactuses. One day during a trip to the zoo, a few months before she died, when Ninon was sixteen, a keeper placed a small capuchin monkey in Louise's arms: she hugged the animal so tightly that it was overcome by panic, struggled, let out sharp screams, but she stubbornly refused to let go, grabbed its hands and, as she did with humans, immediately brought them to her face, placed them firmly against her skin, and the contact of the capuchin's fur against her cheeks prompted tears of joy.

This woman who kept herself both at a great distance, isolated by her physiological condition, and in close proximity, her hand always touching others, this descendant of Marie the dancing madwoman, who too had transmitted the curse to her daughter, Esther, after receiving and slowly digesting it, told her granddaughter, on one of her rare days of despondency, in her halting, fumbling voice: if a world war broke out I wouldn't even realize.

Ninon has resumed her distance learning, hopes to get her high school diploma equivalency, her existence still limited to the boundaries of her bedroom, a nocturnal and fragile animal's burrow, appears to have forgotten her previous life, cohabitates with her mother within this slightly depressed and resigned atmosphere—they rarely eat meals together but sometimes will watch an old Western as they smoke two or three menthol cigarettes followed by a pint of vanilla macadamia nut ice cream—is counting on the time that passes for something to happen, lasting acceptance of her condition, including its painful and solitary form, or even recovery, not facilitated by any healer—after a second stab at shamanic trances, which this time had very minimal effects, Ninon abandoned that path too—but through some internal and miraculous movement inside her body, a secret process linked perhaps to the aging of her cells, or to the end of adolescence, who knows, perhaps life repairs itself sometimes, a process of destruction and healing; so Ninon waits.

And the days go by without change, in the same slowed, hazy rhythm, it's been two years now, any contact with water, sheets, clothes still irritates her skin, but it almost feels like the pain is diminishing, gently waning as the days pass, and on occasion Ninon even abandons the uncomfortable stool on which she's gotten into the habit of sitting to read, eat, watch a screen, protecting her skin, and again settles into the living room couch or an easy chair, making use of the armrests.

At first she's sure of nothing, remains guarded, tells herself that this mysterious dilution of her symptoms is merely the pronounced effect of her familiarity with the pain, once so obtrusive and now integrated into her habitual sensations—hunger, thirst, cold, itchy neck, and arms that burn—accepted as an ordinary functioning of her body, a pain that is no longer foreign but intrinsic to her, as though her affliction had eventually fragmented, scattered, become soluble, dust on the skin's surface. And thus familiarity had set in, along with, according to Ninon who now views herself as a cold monster, a growing insensitivity—feelings turned off, emotional capacities shriveled, burnt to ash; so hardened by the experience that the pain itself has dried up like a dead tree.

But it would appear that her symptoms are continuing to diminish, indisputably, objectively, a little more every day, and are now far removed from what Ninon has known.

Over four weeks, a winter month that obliges her to bundle up even though the heat in the apartment is at maximum, it becomes irrefutable that her allodynia has subsided then disappeared. For no reason, without treatment, without warning, without any change in Ninon's life, her affliction vanished as mysteriously as it arrived. One February morning, Ninon doesn't feel any more pain, not a shadow of discomfort, it's dizzying.

Ninon, astounded, can't celebrate at first, on constant alert for her condition's return, keeps checking, rubs her skin with an exfoliating glove, and finally timidly acknowledges the facts after two weeks, not for all that abandoning a certain suspicion—the affliction could always come back.

To the naked eye her skin remains the same, as pale as before, she scrutinizes it under the bright light of a bulb, it's enough to drive a person mad: the onset of healing is as obscure as that of the illness, being healthy as fantastical as being sick.

Is it possible that the disease fizzled out its own? As though its presence in the body—the tension, the burning, the darkness, the silent agitation—had finally been exhausted, as though the sickness had spurted forth like lava from a volcano before naturally going out, ebb and flow, eruption and cooling.

Ninon is no longer in pain.

After all this time, after the countless therapies and treatments, the endless search, the bursts of enthusiasm, the hypotheses, the attempts, the failures, the follies, the despair, the giving up, the shutting down perhaps, Ninon no longer hurts, full stop, that's the way it is, without a word, without a medication, without an electroshock, it's gone, it went away in the end, the body has resumed its normal functioning, its ideal state, an uncustomary state in reality—troubling, not yet euphoric, because what a relief but also how strange to no longer suffer, she has to regain the fluidity of her gestures and movements, which became so cautious, restrained, and measured, she doesn't have to be afraid of being touched anymore, needs to lower her guard, so that life, so limited and restrained up until now, can broaden once more, can abound once again with thousands of possibilities.

Ninon is lost, senses that she'll need time to return to that life—she still hasn't said anything to her mother, it's difficult—spends several days shut up like before in her bedroom to absorb the incredible shock of being healed, to reset, to renounce her allodynia, an identity lost, to forget the pain that had gradually swallowed her whole, that had dictated the shape of her existence, of her body, rendering her temperament darker and keener, that had subjugated her personality, redefined her life, and finally invented a destiny for her, and tragic as it was, it was her misfortune, profound and indivisible from her being, Ninon is overcome by its absence, and this unwanted emotion sends her into a rage, enraged that she developed an almost tender attachment to her pain, and ashamed of that twisted inclination, for healed Ninon is no longer who she once was, is no longer the splendid anomaly, she's about to join the bland, pacified world of individuals in good health, to reintegrate into the community of the living—that's what she'll tell her mother, that's how she'll announce it: joy at her remission, distress at her loss.

Esther Moise listens to the extraordinary news without the slightest surprise, takes her daughter into her arms, can finally hug her without hurting her—and Ninon, embarrassed, allows the embrace—says that's wonderful, sweetheart, I'm so happy, says who knows maybe I'll get better too one day, Esther thinks they're finally going to reconcile, that everything is going to be fine, says I never doubted it, says I'm proud of you, says anything, of what you went through, of how you handled it, she cries, a little, and Ninon finally pulls away, can't share her mother's emotion, tries to force it, nothing comes, her eyes remain dry, and yet she's trembling, feels like vomiting, and now? what's going to happen? emptiness and warmth in her belly, excitement and apprehension, the desire to soar into the air, to release a battle cry; terror, overwhelming.

If Ninon is truly healed, if it's permanent—but how long until she can be sure? let's remain cautious—then nothing is stopping her anymore from returning to school, going to the pool, taking the metro, rock climbing or boxing, rolling in the grass, rubbing up against strangers in bars and on dance floors, pressing her skin against other skin, touching a whole other body, unknown or familiar, animate or inanimate, soft or hard, everything's allowed, it's staggering. She'll have to overcome her anxiety, the fear of no longer knowing how to go about it, of having unlearned how to live in society, she'll have to brave this return to the world and renounce the tranquility of isolation, but there will be air that once again enters her lungs and a rediscovered feeling of lightness—but not innocence because healing doesn't erase everything, doesn't restore your initial state, healing doesn't mean starting over from the beginning, everything identical and preserved; in the meantime, everything's moved.

Healed, it's confirmed day after day, Ninon doesn't reconcile with her mother as hoped, but distances herself even further, a block of sea ice floating away.

Ninon has killed the animal slinking inside of her—her genetic legacy—reduced it to a hide hanging in a dark and dusty corner of her memory, she jumped out of the line of cursed, mad, degenerate women, and swears to herself that she'll never have children.

Ninon made it out, liberated through healing from the family narrative, she leaves her mother behind, mired and from now on alone, without issue; Esther Moise is erased from the shot, silhouette blurry, a tiny figure in the background; she sinks a little more into her work (accepts all overtime), packs of cigarettes (almost two a day now), and nighttime rambles that sometimes conclude in the bedrooms of recent, grizzled divorcés; these men are regulars at her cinema and the bar she frequents, Le Petit Cardinal on Rue Monge, it rarely lasts more than a week or two, they go see movies of course, sometimes a modern painting exhibition in Beaubourg, have a few final drinks, and then the relationship fizzles out without drama, without conflict—and Esther Moise's whole life seems to be reaching a standstill as her daughter's is restored, as it regains speed.

Ninon gets her high school equivalency, the literature track, enrolls in college, majoring in art history and anthropology, makes a few friends, is hired part-time at the Starbucks in the Grands Boulevards neighborhood in the hope of gaining a little financial independence after those months of doctor-hopping financed by her mother, who always paid without batting an eye, happy to concretize her affection a little, perhaps to compensate for some vague guilt.

Life has resumed, the despair of the flesh has dissipated, she's healed, it's been confirmed, established, not by any doctor's solemn and formalized determination, but by the firm and, again, irrational conviction that there won't be a relapse, suspended time has closed in on itself, a small and dense ball, to be preserved like a relic. Life has resumed because the body is made of miraculous, malleable, and forgetful matter that picks up old habits thought to be lost, also because Ninon is again deploying the enraged determination she mobilized to battle her pain; she's reviving it now so she can heal completely, so she can return to the world, and it's a struggle to once more take an interest in things and in others, to convince herself that being with people is better than being alone, that discussions around a café table are better than the internet and the meanderings of her own brain. Ninon tries to get her youth back through proximity with other young people, hoping that her exact age will manifest itself through capillary action, that the twenty years old she is on paper will take hold of her body, that she'll rediscover the desire to go out, talk, drink, love, socialize.

But neither college—which doesn't feel very intense—nor her casual job at Starbucks—paid next to nothing to make endless macchiatos and lattes at weird hours—really excite her, her friendships remain superficial, limited to lecture halls and the cafeteria. If she listened to her gut, Ninon would go back to staying in her room; she tires quickly, feels distant, separated by a fog, nonetheless forces herself to resume the shared and fluid rhythm of daily life. She's gamely gained some color and a few pounds, her posture's straightened, she bought herself some new, tight clothes, clingy sweaters and form-fitting T-shirts, willingly goes out for drinks after class, tries to participate somewhat in conversations, about professors with old-fashioned ideas or the right-leaning policies of the socialist prime minister, quieting her anxiety, masking a persistent disconnect—a serious, secretive girl, but also composed and attentive, that's how others see her, giving up on piercing Ninon's opaqueness, which is quickly absorbed by the collective flow, and the commotion of drinkers when the clock rings happy hour.

Despite her consistent and sincere efforts, and the relief at her recovery, a suspect emotion never leaves Ninon: unexpected unease, warped dissatisfaction, it's difficult to name, and it's growing.

At night, when she gets home, Ninon will often undress and, standing topless in front of the mirror, observe the skin on her arms, rediscovered skin that she pulls, rubs, strokes, pinches, massages, nibbles, coats with scented lotion; she can't get over it. And like amputees tortured by their absent limbs, their missing and yet intrusive arms, Ninon remains obsessed with her old pain, haunted by its ghost, a hazy shadow that's fading but whose memory, after everything she endured, she'd like to keep. The fact that her pain was so powerful and enormous, a many-tentacled beast, that it sucked out the marrow of her existence for so long, and that today nothing's left, no aftereffects, not a sign, not a fragment to conserve, is to Ninon incomprehensible, and ultimately outrageous. How could her skin, this parchment on which the whole of a life is written, fail to record the dramatic episode that was her allodynia?

It's as if the void left by her pain had to be filled, as if some new source of intensity was demanding to be activated, as though she had to conserve proof of the ferocity and disproportionality of her experience.

The feeling that she hasn't been amputated of a limb but of her pain is a form of madness hanging over Ninon's head, and she knows she better protect herself.

And so Ninon decides to get tattooed.

Imagines it as a remedy for what's not quite right inside of her, for that feeling of incompletion, for her obsessional tendencies.

Naked again, in front of her mirror, she studies her hips that have widened, her round breasts perched high on her chest, her flat, slightly concave stomach, her smooth, homogenous, virgin skin, and her cumbersome arms, which hang on either side of her body and give her a bumbling air.

The idea of tattooing as a possible denouement had taken root long before, perhaps even when this strange story of skin first began, a hidden and as-yet inaccessible idea idling in the back of her mind, a vague desire waiting to be triggered and that from now on will connect to everything that's happened to her, everything that keeps happening to her because something is still missing.

Tattooing as a magic portal back to a normal social but also biological life, to repair the friction, the chasm that isn't diminishing, the insistent void. Getting her arms tattooed, a brilliant, comforting thought, will be Ninon's revenge: thwart her body's amnesia—her skin can't remember the pain but it will be covered in ink in memoriam—and rebuild her identity: new skin, new start.

And also because tattoos are beautiful and Ninon has been deprived of beauty for so long, of the possibility of rejoicing in beauty.

Once again Ninon turns to the internet in search of her salvation, a way in, an answer, there are hundreds of tattoo parlors, she studies the photos, rules out places with cold interiors, tile floors, flashy neon signs, biker and goth types, she doesn't need a tattoo artist experienced with subtle, delicate strokes, dotwork on sensitive areas, or meticulous shading, because she's not considering a tribal motif or Chinese ideogram, nor a mandala, dragon, pin-up girl, snake wrapped around a dagger, ship anchor, or plump rose, no butterfly, cross on her back, lion on her lower stomach, dream catcher on her shoulder blade, rising sun on her wrist, mermaid, or swallow, no keys or clasping hands, not a drawing or a word, no dates or names, no incorrectly spelled quotes or Latin maxims, no carpe diem and no "4-eva." And for that matter what design or phrase could a person stand forever, endure for as long as the body hangs on, withering and growing pale with it?

Ninon knows exactly what she wants, knew it right away, without hesitation: to cover her entire arms with black ink, from the wrists to where the shoulders begin, so that the tattoo forms two long protective sleeves, a second skin inked onto her white skin, a flat tint that renders the original envelope invisible. She can already imagine the bold beauty of her blackened arms extending from her pale body, a stranger's arms, a discordant presence. Ninon recalls a striking photo of Daniel Darc, the French post-punk rocker, taken just before his death, his inked arms proudly brandished before the lens—that's what she wants. Daniel Darc's body tattoo covered a multitude of older tattoos, acquired over time then regretted no doubt, as they became inappropriate, or even unbearable. But whereas Daniel Darc wanted to hide, to forget what came before, Ninon plans on the contrary to show every inch of her liberated skin.

She eventually picks a tattoo parlor run by three young women, near Pigalle, with light-colored wood floors and walls covered with 1970s movie posters. You go to the parlor to meet the tattooers—their attitude: surly—explain what you want, test your motivation, schedule an appointment for two months later, and make a deposit.

The tattoo artist who meets with Ninon is a tall blond in tight jeans and a Nirvana T-shirt, her arms striped with thin black lines that go all the way to her neck. Multiple dots and dashes decorate her fingers (one dot: freedom; three dots: death to pigs), the palm of her right hand is tattooed with a ruby-red heart pierced by an arrow, her left palm with an owl, a tiny rhombus is stamped between her eyes, and a third eye has been drawn, engraved almost, on her neck—an eye, she says, looking out for her own death; she's maybe thirty years old.

The tattoo artist questions Ninon about her choice, is surprised at how radical this first tattoo is, an unusual request from such a young woman, worries about regrets to come. But Ninon is sure of herself, impatient, excited by the thought of this irreversible act.

The tattoo artist explains that it will require a dozen three-hour sessions over several weeks, that it will be expensive, and that it will be painful. Ninon will pay using the two thousand and six hundred euros she saved working at Starbucks, and can certainly pilfer another four hundred euros from her mother's various hiding places.

The tattoo artist concludes by telling her not to show up with an empty stomach, to avoid drinking or taking drugs the night before, and, last thing, asks Ninon if she's pregnant. Ever since she heard about the American woman who got tattooed when she was six months along and supposedly gave birth three months later to an inked-out newborn—the infant's skin bore the same marks as its mother's: blue ivy and the head of a red bird—the tattoo artist has refused to take a similar risk, aware that this preventive measure sounds ridiculous, but you never know, the female body is unfathomable.

At the first session Ninon is nervous, though determined, though accustomed to pain, she wonders what this new kind of pain might feel like, how intense will it be, whether she'll be able to bear it in silence.

The tattoo artist has Ninon lie down on a massage table covered by a paper sheet and prepares her work space: surgically disinfects her hands, uses Lysol to sterilize the metallic tray, which will be wrapped in cellophane, preps the coil tattoo machine, opens a bag of sterile needles and ink capsules, then the Vaseline, lubricant, and black latex gloves, vigorously cleans Ninon's arms, we'll start with the left one if that's okay—a long aseptic ritual that carries a bitter reminder of Ninon's past medical consultations.

The tattoo artist places Ninon's arm on an armrest, also disinfected, points the magnifying lamp at her skin, moves closer, eye-level, settles onto a rolling stool, launches the tattoo machine by pressing the transformer pedal—the buzzing of an electrical insect, a large mechanical bee, a strident vibration—then, quill in hand, dips it delicately into the tiny capsule of black ink, ready Ninon? let's get started.

The tattoo artist works to music, a long playlist of electronica and soul that doesn't completely mask the high-pitched and ultimately irritating hum of the tattoo machine; Ninon watches her: tense, forehead wrinkled and soon covered by a thin veil of sweat, twisting around her subject's arm, pausing periodically to see how the skin is reacting, wiping away any dripping ink, any black liquid disgorged by the epidermis, which is more or less porous, receptive, more or less impermeable depending on the area, to reassure herself that the ink is being absorbed, to catch her breath too, to maintain her concentration, and to give Ninon a second—you ok? can I keep going?

Ninon had imagined a stinging pain, beneath the machine's needles, but the instrument doesn't sting, it burns, a diffuse burning sensation, like the flame of a lighter licking the surface of her arms—a thin blade of fire cutting into the skin—similar to the fire of allodynia, which awakens that distant memory though without violence, gently almost, a reconciliation with pain, which has been reactivated, summoned, so it can finally be dominated. Ninon observes with satisfaction her body darken, colored dot by dot.

After two hours, they take a break to relax their muscles, the tattoo artist's sore neck, Ninon's tingling hand, to smoke a cigarette, clear their minds with some fresh air, appreciate the shiny tinge to the ink newly dispersed through the skin—soon it will sink into the epidermis, lose its black sheen, and turn matte and bluish.

When they get back to it, Ninon is completely relaxed, slightly inebriated by the endorphins her brain is producing under the assault of the tattoo needles, she no longer hears the tool's annoying crackling, her thoughts float through the tiny tattoo parlor, perching like chickadees on the music's bass lines, she wishes the anesthetizing pain could last, a cocoon, a capsule, but she's also in a hurry, to see her arms completely covered, impatient at the idea that it will take many more hours, feels idiotically and vaguely proud, of all of this, of such a long story that began in childhood, of the centuries wrapped up in her twenty years, of this chosen metamorphosis, a self-contamination.

After a session of three hours, the tattoo artist's eyes are glazed, her wrist aches, Ninon is dazed and happy, she marvels at the menacing black stain that's begun to colonize her skin, stretching below her shoulder, she's only thinking of one thing, resuming as quickly as possible; they have to wait two weeks for the swelling in her arm to go down, for all the bleeding to stop.

The tattoo creates an immediate addiction in Ninon, an addiction to a very specific pain, one that doesn't make you suffer, enduring it is a victory, gentle euphoria, and Ninon, once so vulnerable, feels full of strength.

The now-tattooed Ninon has finally made her body yield—this body that revived her anxiety every morning upon waking, delivering cruel reminders of its presence and of the fact that the second she opened her eyes, she'd need to again occupy a burning physical casing, this pitiless, irremediable, intransigent body that she'd have liked to leave behind, racing ahead and never turning around, in order to find herself somewhere it wasn't, projected, untouchable, into another universe, this body that every day made its weighty presence known, inflicting the same wound, a never-ending punishment, the enemy feigning friendship, the tyrant that corners us, forces us to submit, at times humiliates us. This time it's she who triumphs, and it's so rare to see this omnipotent body that we helplessly inhabit capitulate. It feels like revenge and like a miracle, like power and freedom, and Ninon would be willing to tattoo her whole body to experience this again and again.

*

The tattoo artist coats Ninon's skin with a pungent antiseptic fluid, wraps her arm in a large sheet of cellophane, hands her a tube of healing ointment to apply morning and night for two weeks, warns her that it might itch, not to scratch, and to let flakes of dead skin gradually fall off in the shower.

O ne of the last and most beautiful chapters of the genealogical narrative, a particularly fantastical episode in the
family saga, enthusiastically recounted by Esther, brings Ninon's
great-grandmother onto the scene.

Though Ninon was only four when Rose Flanchet died, she
still remembers her burnt skin and its mysterious markings that
came from the sky. Whenever the old woman sat her granddaughter on her knees, Ninon would try to unbutton Rose's shirt
and pull off her sweater to reveal a faded, imprinted décolleté, to
trace with her little chubby finger the lines and curves of tattoos
drawn by lightning.

Married to a forest ranger in the Vercors mountains, Rose
Flanchet was in the habit of accompanying her husband on his
rounds between the Écouges range and the forest of Léoncel,
walking for miles every day with her dog and her stick, keeping

an eye out for black grouses and ptarmigans, an outdoors woman with muddy boots, a gourd of water, and a photo of her children in a medallion worn directly against her skin—this is how Ninon's mother described her—a woman a little more liberated than most at the beginning of the twentieth century, accustomed to monitoring the clouds and being wary of storms, frequent in the region, and who was caught by surprise by a bolt of lightning.

And yet Rose Flanchet knew everything you need to know about thunderstorms: that when wind, black clouds, and hail appear, you should in no case take shelter beneath a tree or inside a cave, that you should stay away from fences and ridges, that you shouldn't brandish metallic objects above your head, or stand with your legs spread, or walk briskly, and that you should curl up on the ground in a little ball—she knew all of that but still allowed the lightning to come to her.

Rose Flanchet had always managed to dodge that menace from above, even though she lived surrounded by spruces and beech trees, she knew what Nature was like when enraged, knew the sky's erratic movements, knew how to distinguish between the linear bolts of staccato, forked, and bead lightning; and her dog always smelled the electricity in the air several hours before a storm began, fur bristling at the first distant discharges announcing the disaster in store.

*

But that day, as thunderclaps rumbled and the sky was ripped apart, Rose, having chosen to go for a walk alone, remained frozen beneath the pounding rain, head tilted back to drink the black storm water, ecstatic, oblivious to the danger and violence, scorning the lightning that, as she knew, often kills, attracted like a magnet to all living things, that creeps beneath clothes, beneath the skin, that burns the eyes, consumes fur and hair, scorches beards, and tumefies the sexual organs.

Rose had seen storm victims before: a man struck down, his head swollen and temples perforated, another whose body was carbonized, reduced to ash, and even the dark silhouette of a poor shepherd etched into the wall of the sheepfold in front of which he had dropped dead. She also knew that lightning has strange, supernatural effects, that it had burnt a road mender's hand down to the bone while leaving his leather glove intact, that once, quite the opposite, it had disintegrated another's shoe without touching his foot, that it was also capable of undressing its victims—in which case, one found shredded items of clothing scattered a few feet away—that it had struck a pregnant woman who gave birth a few hours later to a baby whose body had been broiled, like a chicken kebab, that it interrupts young girls' menstruation, sometimes for good, and brings back that of menopausal women, that it causes a multitude of ailments and that countless laughable or horrendous stories are told about it.

Lightning is driven by subtle intentions, it chooses its victim with precision, designating its target with a ball of fire or spurt of light—there's not a man or woman in the whole of the Vercors who doesn't know that, not a forest ranger's wife who didn't learn to beware lightning as if it were the plague, and yet, Rose Flanchet stood beneath a pine tree, she didn't take shelter, didn't make any of the basic protective poses, she waited for the fire, defied the lightning, perhaps she thought herself untouchable, this woman of the forest who had escaped dozens of thunderstorms, who knew every tree, stone, and bird in this mountain range, she decided to confront the tempest, spread her legs, raised her arms toward the dark sky, a somber, drenched velvet tapestry, her dog howled, curled up in a ball at her feet, no longer recognizing its owner, and the lightning hit with a resounding din that pierced the animal's eardrums, it struck the woman who felt astounding pressure between her shoulder blades, down her spine, as if the entire forest had collapsed on her back, and she lost consciousness.

Rose Flanchet wasn't found until the next morning, still uncon-scious, collapsed beneath her tree, the now-deaf dog watching over her, someone checked her pulse, she was alive, they carried her on a stretcher to her small house built of shingles and stone, the doctor summoned to her bedside had her undressed. He had already cared for women and men struck by lightning, skin burnt and bruised, covered with blisters, falling off in shreds, he had observed macules and bleeding rosettes through his magnifying glass, but he had never seen anything this remarkable.

Rose's torso and breasts bore the outlines of the tree under which she had been standing when the lightning struck. You could clearly make out the trunk, branches, and the texture of the bark. At first, the doctor thought that the lightning had thickened the blood in her vessels, rendering them visible beneath the skin, bold tracks that might bring to mind the shape of a tree. But the lines didn't diminish as the hours went by, in fact they stood out even more distinctly, it could only be an image etched by the lightning itself onto a body that had become a hypersensitive surface—the forest's incendiary aura.

Rose was then turned onto her stomach, revealing additional imprints on the other side of her body: leaves, beech branches, ferns. The outlines were brown, dry, lovely curving strokes, slightly raised, by roughly one millimeter; her back was literally the negative of the forest.

But the biggest surprise came a few days later with the appearance of three new markings, in the shape of a coin and a small knife that had been in the bottom of the front pocket of Rose's apron and of the medallion she wore around her neck, whose outlines, though less distinct than those of the trees, were now entirely visible and identifiable. The imprinting of these metallic and conductive objects was undoubtedly easier to explain, but there was no indication as to why these marks formed so late, surfacing from deep beneath the skin.

This was how Esther Moise told her daughter Ninon about the way in which Nature had left its mark of authority on her great-grandmother's vulnerable body. She also described how proud Rose Flanchet had always been of her tattoos, a sign, in her mind, of having been "chosen." Rose recovered from the shock in a few days, had no aftereffects other than her epidermal drawings, became famous in the region, had her picture taken, spoke about the incident in public, allowed the doctors to take a few samples of her skin and test its acidity, and from then on loved stormy weather and overcast skies even more than before but never again exposed herself to lightning, fearful perhaps that a second bolt would make her tattoos disappear as mysteriously as they had appeared.

For the rest of her life, Rose was fascinated by other extraordinary cases found in scientific literature; faithful to the family record-keeping tradition, she listed them in a notebook, which was handed down to her granddaughter, Esther: for example, the story of a sailor on his ship during a thunderstorm who recognized, imprinted on his arm, the horseshoe he had nailed to the mast a few hours earlier. Or more astounding still, the story of the struck-down sheep. As they crossed a meadow in the woods, the animals were surprised by a storm and several in the flock were killed by lightning. Following the tragic event, the shepherd decided to shear his animals to salvage their wool and meat; he then discovered that inside the skin of every dead sheep, once the bits of flesh were washed off, was what looked to be an engraving of the surrounding countryside—and together, every sheep laid next to the other recreated, in panorama, the entire landscape. You could recognize the slopes in the terrain, species of trees, embankments, and possibly even the shapes of the clouds.

The memory of this great-grandmother, this ancestress tattooed by fire, recorded in the outrageous history of a family that has always favored fantasy over reason, exceptionalism over logic, aspiring to stand out, is now coming back to Ninon in the form of a fairy tale that is both dark and gay, like a distant sign— someone else marked skin-deep and who got a happy ending.

Ninon begins her second session full of energy, her thirsty skin has imbibed the ink and healed nicely, the black pigment has settled, perfectly smooth. The first few days, she would look at her arm in fascination, exhilarated by what she'd done, though there was the occasional burst of panic.

The tattoo artist had warned her, the tattoo will provoke a feeling of immense satisfaction at first, then, if you don't regret it, you'll quickly forget about it, after a week you won't even see it, and Ninon did quickly forget, disappointed to find that such an intense emotion could recede in so little time, impatient to return to that early state of inebriation, and sensing that this emotional seesaw would be endless, a milder version of the drug addict's frenzied quest, constantly starting over to attain the same feverish excitement that you couldn't make last.

The ritual to prepare the work space is the same, just a different soundtrack, mainly hip-hop this time, and they're off for three hours of tattooing, the needle slowly moving down Ninon's arm, the now familiar, almost pleasant, pain, the silence between them, the trust, one deep in concentration, the other's thoughts roaming.

During the cigarette break, the tattoo artist shares her fondest memory, the story of a fifty-year-old client whose chest she tattooed following a mastectomy: after surviving breast cancer, the woman had come in to get a series of tattoos that would camouflage her surgical scars, she had chosen flowers and tangled brambles, a bird, a colorful butterfly, and a ladybug in place of a nipple, like a garden of Eden, a lost paradise that would flourish where her breasts had disappeared. A commemorative plaque, too, a memento mori. Rather than turning to reconstructive surgery, rather than getting breast implants, because she wasn't that keen on them, or maybe because she couldn't afford them, this woman had chosen to replace, or symbolize, her chest with decorative tattoos, to hide an absence as much as to reveal it.

Ninon immediately imagines the amputated woman's tattoos as war paintings, the drawings on her body as an act of defiance, as provocation and protection, pictures a daring woman, her embellished chest attracting all the attention on the beach, inspiring marvel and apprehension, respect and fear, a woman trying to make the most out of what life has inflicted on her—something was taken away so she adds something, a tattoo that becomes an organ—a woman who fixes herself, a surgeon in her own right, she cobbles together a new body, a prosthesis of ink instead of silicone, a mutant who chose her mutation—to forget but also not to. And Ninon, by getting tattooed, wants her body to remember in this same paradoxical way: the skin records life, the tattoo archives it, then covers everything.

Ninon remembers that at the height of her pain she would have begged a surgeon to amputate her arms, to take away that unbearable bodily presence; now she plans to wave them in the world's face, to parade her tragic body.

She waits impatiently for each new session, a repeated celebration, a calming ritual; from week to week, month to month, she observes one arm then the other turning black, and as her skin is increasingly contaminated, she imagines the ink strengthening it, strengthening her body's envelope by doubling it, like a thin neoprene suit, a membrane of pigments that forms an impassable shield, she visualizes every pore on her skin filling with ink, the tattoo protects her, the tattoo might have protected her from allodynia, a medicinal, prophylactic tattoo that might have repelled the assaults of the disease; it might have eased the pain once her condition manifested because—this is what the tattoo artist tells her and Ninon can't believe that none of the doctors or healers she saw suggested this kind of treatment—a tattoo is also a remedy, it's used similarly to acupuncture or minor surgery, dots, lines, and crosses are traced onto the painful area, drawings that follow the nerves' path, a hidden anatomical network, and facilitate, divert, or block the circulation of fluids and lymphatic humors.

After ten three-hour sessions, Ninon's two arms are tattooed from shoulder to wrist, on both sides, her white hands draw the gaze—two small creatures wriggling at the end of black forearms that resemble boa constrictors—they seem even paler, almost sickly-looking, and that strangeness delights Ninon.

Looking in the mirror, she admires her new nudity, her splendid duotonality, a peculiarity that gives her confidence, she feels it, her blue-veined untouched skin from which emerge these two defiant and Luciferian arms of ebony, the arms of a witch, an impressive dark/light.

Esther Moise, who only sees, knows, and likes the world in black and white, again takes her daughter in her arms—this has become her only available language—you're so beautiful, and interprets this crazy tattoo as a sign, a step in her direction, to pick up the thread of the story perhaps.

But though Ninon allows the hug, her thoughts, agitated by the tattoo sessions, carry her somewhere else, toward another, chosen, family, another lineage, this one horizontal, transversal. Ninon, healed from the curse, bolstered by her new skin, now dreams of a different history, fantasizes about a new bloodline, imagines she's the child, or sister rather, of the sailors who, to kill time during their long crossings, tattooed each other with rudimentary tools—five needles attached to the end of a piece of wood—and makeshift pigments, vermillion and India ink, black ash or cacao, and eau-de-vie for cleaning. Imagines brothers for herself in the convicts and criminals tattooing themselves in their jail cells with shards of glass or sharp stones and bits of chipped brick, disinfecting their skin with saliva or urine. Imagines brothers in the delinquents who defied the Church's interdiction—you shall not modify your God-given body—who practiced the art of tattooing, with sloppy, unattractive results, in a dark workshop, beneath a staircase, in the backroom of a café, cutting their skin with a broken scallop shell coated with ink. Imagines brothers in the soldiers of France's North African battalions, the Bat' d'Af, redemptive combat units composed of military conscripts with long criminal records, somber men covered with military and patriotic emblems, names of cities and boats, sexual references on their lower stomachs—"bushwhacker"—melancholy or vengeful messages alluding to a woman's betrayal or endured humiliations and violence—"death to unfaithful women," "child of misfortune." And imagines sisters in those first tattooed women: prostitutes, circus artists, members of Parisian street gangs, female pirates, and "bad girls."

Ninon imagines herself related to all them, a list of kin she compiles in silence, as her mother finally loosens her grip, can picture herself leaving her world, joining those who invent identities temporarily embedded in their skin, and which will die with them, disintegrating in coffins as their bodies rot, returning to dust and mold, skin crumbling like paper, joining those who she imagines live with no thought to transmission or heritage, without continuity or horizon.

And so the act of getting tattooed had this fantastically exaggerated, and no doubt ludicrous and fleeting, effect on Ninon, which one would imagine was due to her youth and what she's been through, amplified as much as it is excusable: far from interrupting the much denigrated fiction-spinning wheel, the abhorred book of family tales, Ninon begins another self-narrative, it's her turn to create an identity for herself, that of a tattooed girl and proud of it, viewing it as a way to weaken her original identity, which she imagines dissolving in the ink, growing smaller beneath the needles. Ninon, who had long reproached her mother for telling herself stories, does the same thing, stories of self-begetting and emancipation, even devises a plan to erase herself entirely, to tattoo herself down to her fingertips, to mask and muddle her prints—but skin can't be erased, Ninon, it marks you for life, you can aspire to a less inglorious identity, you can burn the pads of your fingers, submerge them in a bath of fire and acid, your fingerprints will always grow back, reforming again and again, and you'll remain Ninon Moise, daughter of Esther Moise.

Ninon found Jeremy on Tinder, she downloaded the app on her iPhone a few days after her final tattoo session, wanted to meet someone quickly, have sex as soon as possible, not bother with long conversations in a coffee shop, the buildup and drag-it-out phases. Given those terms, Tinder is the most rewarding and most direct hook-up technique, a photo, a location on a map, a finger swiping right to say "I like you," left to ignore someone's profile; if they coincide, you exchange a few messages and set up a nearby meeting. That's exactly what Ninon wanted, she'd waited too long already, liked the idea that Tinder allows two envelopes of skin to find each other easily in the same geographical zone, she found it clever and efficient, another emancipatory tool, fingers crossed that the bodies are satisfied.

They meet at the Café des Anges near Place Clichy at six p.m.; Jeremy is twenty-two years old and pleases Ninon from the start: lanky, with strawberry-blond hair, slightly wide-set eyes, a rhinestone in his right ear, he's pursuing a master's in sociology, exudes a smell of lemony cologne and a gentle manner—ideal for a first time.

Sitting in the back of the restaurant, they drink, him beer, her vodka-tonic to build courage, and to impress him. They exchange a few dozen sentences about their respective studies, the bars in their shared neighborhood, PNL's latest album, then the conversation lags; they look at other in silence, but without awkwardness, know that they like each other, that it's only a matter of time, the time they impose, that they deem decent, appropriate, before heading out, maybe another half hour of chatting, and they'll go up to Jeremy's tiny attic studio on Rue Saint-Lazare, around the corner. Then, it's a mild April, Ninon takes off her sweater, it's warm in here, that's how she reveals her tattooed arms which Jeremy greets with a surprised and admiring wow, receptive to the black pigment's erotic charge, and in fact he gets a hard-on, hidden under the bistro table.

He doesn't ask anything about the stirring discovery, just: well, should we go? And then their movements accelerate, some cash thrown on the table, Jeremy's hand around Ninon's waist, she doesn't push it away, a few minutes later they're taking the stairs two by two to the seventh floor, racing into the studio, grabbing each other, kissing each other—Ninon's bumbling tongue, a stranger almost, a small flailing animal, then its rotations grow more fluid, it clings to Jeremy's elastic, supple tongue, the bitter taste of beer— they hurry to undress, a little clumsily, a sneaker heel that gets stuck, a stubborn jean button, a T-shirt that's too tight, Ninon doesn't tell Jeremy it's her first time, she says nothing, prepares herself, isn't scared at all, finally they're naked on the sofa bed, Jeremy on top of Ninon, skin against skin, Jeremy's is the color of chalk verging on pale pink, sprinkled with freckles, the veins are very visible, you can follow their path on the insides of his arms, he smells of invigorating shower gel, cold tobacco, and garlic.

Ninon's skin warms in contact with Jeremy's, sprouts red halos, but her arms remain cold, as though the blackness is protecting them, isolating them from heat, pushing back the light; and within this embrace Ninon can clearly sense the disparity in temperature, her arms once again standing out, prominent, instead of melting into the act, the sensation is annoying, upsetting, and Ninon repels it by kissing Jeremy even harder, inviting him to go even deeper—a sharp but brief pain, like a dry twig cracking, and Ninon, short of breath, is happy.

*

They've gotten partially dressed and slid beneath the sheets, smoking post-sex cigarettes like in the movies, sweet-flavored Amsterdamer rolling tobacco, trying to blow smoke rings out of puckered mouths, Jeremy wraps his arm around Ninon's neck, so tell me the story with your tattoo.

Ninon doesn't mention her family, allodynia, or her recovery, but happily talks about her proud tattoo, the hours spent under the needle, the only reasons she gives are her desire, the beauty and strangeness, and that suffices for Jeremy, under the spell, who wonders aloud whether he should get a tattoo too, how about here on my shoulder, an octopus maybe, with tentacles that would wrap around my bicep. He strokes Ninon's arm like it's velvet, marvels at the depth of the black, it's crazy what you did, Ninon, we'll see each other again I hope.

They sleep intertwined for one hour, it's well into evening when they wake up, they smoke again in bed and open cans of beer, dig into bags of chips, talk a little, about protests and Facebook—and nothing in Ninon's words or sometimes evasive responses betrays her, betrays her months, her years of isolation, the gulf in her existence, now closed, the illusion is perfect, a girl like any other and an ordinary life.

They have sex again, very quickly, drunk on beer and everything else, and as Ninon's dozing off, Jeremy turns toward her, propped up on one elbow, bends over her ear, since you like tattoos so much, Ninon, listen to this, you're gonna love it. And as if to lull her to sleep, he whispers a story:

It takes place on Banaba Island in the Pacific Ocean, a tiny island measuring less than four square miles and inhabited by three hundred Banabans, and which is surrounded by a coral reef barrier and covered in phosphate deposits. Birds nesting in the surrounding rocks would shit in the water, and those droppings eventually petrified inside the reef and turned into phosphate. That means the island of Banaba sits on a foundation of bird excrement, layers upon layers that eventually emerged at sea level.

But I'm telling you about the Banabans because they practice the art of tattooing. They carve large needles out of almond tree wood or tortoise shells, which they dip into a thick ink made from coconut ashes mixed with salt and diluted in water. Their bodies are completely covered with tattoos, head included, and it's always the same simple, repetitive designs, lines and curves that turn into feathers.

Once they're tattooed, the Banabans are ready for death, ready for the afterlife. Their dead bodies aren't buried, or burned, or cast to sea, they're displayed outside. The island-ers wait patiently for the skin to rot, for the skeleton to emerge, then they wash the corpse and bury the bones and the skull separately. And here's where it gets interesting, Ninon, here's where you're concerned—Ninon, eyelids closed, breathing steady, is paying attention—after death, the Banaban's soul leaves its body and flies to the western part of the island, home to a formidable deity, Nei Karamakuna, the bird-headed woman; she stops souls in their path, demands sustenance in return for the right of passage—Jeremy knows it's working, Ninon opens her eyes, shuts them again—and tattoos are what Nei Karamakuna feeds on.

The bird-headed woman eats the drawings etched into the skin of the dead, she rips them out with her beak, sucks up the ink, and once she's full shows her gratitude by allowing these souls to continue on their way, and most importantly by offering them new eyes, as keen as a ghost's, a new sense of sight that will allow the departed to move around in the afterlife.

But what happens to those without tattoos, Ninon? What terrible fate awaits them? Furious at being deprived of food, the bird-headed woman jabs out their eyes with her sharp beak. The non-tattooed, now blind, are doomed to be forever lost within the twists and turns of hell.

And what about you, Ninon, are you preparing for your journey into the afterlife? If you meet the bird-headed woman after you die, your arms will be enough to satiate her for centuries, she'll guzzle down all that ink stored in your skin, you'll have earned your new eyes, you'll see clearer than anyone in the land of darkness.

C'mon, let's get some sleep, I have class later, Jeremy dozes off immediately whereas Ninon, eyes wide open, fully alert, fully awakened by the legend of the Banabans, is spinning into her fantasy world. She had reinvented herself as a tattooed hooligan, and now, enveloped by this Parisian night, this attic studio, these warm sheets, she imagines her grand migration to Banaba Island to meet the bird-headed woman. Ninon will never escape the power of myths, she'll continue seeking a narrative she can cling to, or melt into, something to say about her life because no experience is pure, no experience exists without a story, Ninon is a little lost, she's molting, leaving her old skin behind, the ancestral envelope, she tore it off herself, in search of herself, shaking it loose so she can grab onto something else, make other voluntary connections, find other holds; but she can't completely let go, can't erase her memories or attain absolute solitude, neither the abolition of time nor spontaneous generation are possible.

*

JOY SORMAN

Ninon Moise, twenty years old, was brought into this world, grew up, got sick, got better, got tattooed, knew love, and now the sun is peeking into the studio skylight, the sky is brightening, the song of a blackbird, the pneumatic motor of a trash truck, Jeremy's deep breathing beside her, footsteps in the hallway, the first cars in the distance, the dull thump of her heart beating a little too fast, more blackbirds then sparrows, the digital alarm clock goes off—short and long pulses like a message in Morse code—a ray of sunlight on the bed, on her black, matte arms extending from the sheet, a faint feeling of warmth on her skin, fragments of voices rising from the street to the seventh floor, paint peeling on the ceiling and a bare bulb, brown water rings, scattered clothes, the smell of coffee coming from elsewhere, a board on a trestle weighed down by books and empty cans, the computer screen in sleep mode—colorful spirals—a small foam armchair, a cellphone vibrating behind the party wall, a microwave on a high stool, someone yells, a black-and-white photo of Paris crookedly tacked up, the sound of a door being locked, squealing tires and car horns, Jeremy grunts—a raspy cough—a barking dog, the sun's all the way up, a clear day, and a pungent smell inside this room, beer, cold tobacco, sperm and sweat mixed, bodies exuding something—life, life, life, thinks Ninon, lifting the covers with a broad motion, revealing her nude, brave body; life, clearly.

JOY SORMAN is a novelist and documentarian based in Paris. Her first novel, *Boys, boys, boys*, was awarded the 2005 Prix de Flore. In 2013, she received the Prix François Mauriac from the Académie française for *Comme une bête*.

LARA VERGNAUD is a literary translator of prose, creative nonfiction, and scholarly works from the French. She is the recipient of two PEN/Heim Translation Fund Grants and a French Voices Grand Prize, and has been nominated for the National Translation Award.

CATHERINE LACEY is a Guggenheim fellow, a Whiting Award winner, and the author of four works of fiction: *Nobody Is Ever Missing*, *The Answers*, *Certain American States*, and *Pew*.

RESTLESS BOOKS is an independent, nonprofit publisher devoted to championing essential voices from around the world whose stories speak to us across linguistic and cultural borders. We seek extraordinary international literature for adults and young readers that feeds our restlessness: our hunger for new perspectives, passion for other cultures and languages, and eagerness to explore beyond the confines of the familiar.

Through cultural programming, we aim to celebrate immigrant writing and bring literature to underserved communities. We believe that immigrant stories are a vital component of our cultural consciousness; they help to ensure awareness of our communities, build empathy for our neighbors, and strengthen our democracy.

Visit us at restlessbooks.org